James E. Cherry is a southern-born black man. He experienced a spiritual, mental and cultural awakening in his mid-twenties, which inspired him to become a writer. *Shadow of Light* is his first novel. A poet as well, he is the author of a chapbook, *Bending the Blues* (H&H Press) and will release a full collection of verse, *Honoring the Ancestors,* in the fall of 2008 from Third World Press. He lives in Tennessee.

SHADOW OF LIGHT

James E. Cherry

A complete catalogue record for this book can be obtained from
the British Library on request

First published in 2007 by Serpent's Tail,
an imprint of Profile Books Ltd
3A Exmouth House
Pine Street
London EC1R 0JH
website: www.serpentstail.com

ISBN 978 1 85242 492 3

Designed and typeset by Mathew Lyons

Printed in the UK by CPI Bookmarque, Croydon, CR0 4TD

10 9 8 7 6 5 4 3 2 1

Shadow of Light is dedicated to Richard Wright, Chester B. Himes and John A. Williams whose literary harvests I continue to reap.

A book is like a man—clever and dull, brave and cowardly, beautiful and ugly. For every flowering thought there will be a page like a wet and mangy mongrel and for every looping flight a tap on the wing and a reminder that wax cannot hold the feathers firm too near the sun.

John Steinbeck

"**PULL OVER HERE, MAN**. This where the bitch live."

Tony eased the '74 Impala to the side of the road, skidding to a stop in a cloud of loose gravel, dust and the humidity of Saturday night.

"I don't think I want no part of this, man," Tony said, gripping the steering wheel with both hands, his blond hair plastered to his head from sweat and trepidation. Jamie sat in the passenger seat beside him; Lee and Ronny in the back.

Tony felt a hard cold pressure at the back of his skull that caused his teeth to chatter as if it was the middle of January as opposed to the end of August.

"Whatcha think now?" Ronny held a loaded .38 to Tony's head. "I always knew you was a pussy, Tony. Didn't I tell you guys that if anything happen, he'd be the one to rat on us. Huh?"

Tony held both hands in the air, surrendering all resistance.

"Ronny, what are you doing!" screamed Lee.

"What the hell it looks like I'm doing? I'm about to make up this motherfucker's mind for him."

Jamie stretched his arm over the back of the front seat, trying to occupy as much space as possible between himself and Ronny. "Ron? Ronny. Take it easy, man. Ain't nothing changed." Jamie's voice was quiet and reassuring, the way you placate a dog with bared teeth and menacing growl. "If he wanna leave, let him. We're gonna do what we gotta do. We've been planning this for weeks now, remember? Tony's cool. Just put the gun down."

Ronny cocked the hammer of the handgun and the sound of crickets, the call of an owl and the collective breath of the whole world seemed to converge and suspend itself inside of the blue four-door sedan. Ronny's eyes glazed over into a vacant, maniacal stare, his face twisted into a sneer.

"Put the gun down, Ronny." Jamie's voice exploded the tension, his words slicing the air with shards of authority. He had made up his mind, positioned himself to grab the barrel of the gun and leap simultaneously over the seat to end the ordeal. He knew somebody was going to get shot one way or the other. He just hoped it wouldn't be him.

"C'mon, man!" Lee was cringing in the corner of the back seat with a hand covering his eyes and tears streaming through his fingers. "That's your own brother you pointing a gun at, for crying out loud!"

"So what?" Ronny stated matter of factly. "I should've shot him when I was twelve years old. Four years later is better than never." Then he quickly eased the hammer, lowered the gun and cursed aloud. "What'd you mean 'Ain't nothin' changed?' Where the hell you think he going when he leaves here, Jamie?"

Jamie had known Ronny ever since grade school and even then he was bullying kids twice his size. He knew to show any signs of weakness around Ronny would be like putting a collar around your neck and the leash in his hands. "Why don't you ask him your damn self?"

Jamie and Ronny gawked at one another until Jamie's stare began to bore a hole through Ronny, forcing him to turn away. He blurted, "Where the hell you think you going, faggot?"

Tony mechanically lowered his hands, talked to his younger brother through the rearview mirror. "I'm going over to Kara's, Ronny, that's all. I ain't going to tell nobody nothing."

"You ain't gonna run to the police?"

"Hell, nah!"

You ain't gonna tell Mama?"

"Hell, nah!"

Lee was squirming as if he were sitting on a stack of needles, drying his face with the back of his hand. "Can we cut all this bullshit out and do what we gotta do? You guys are making me crazy." He slammed his head three times on the back of the seat, then rested it there, closing his eyes.

"You know I'ma kill you, boy. If you talk," Ronny said, his voice calm with menace. "No matter how long it takes, Tony. You know I'll hunt you down."

"Yeah, Ronny," Tony replied, no longer looking in the rear mirror. "I hear ya."

Jamie and Ronny stared at one another again, this time with half the amount of intensity, until Ronny exclaimed, "You think you got enough guts to pull into the driveway, my pussy of a brother? And let me tell *you* something," he leveled the gun at Lee's head, "if you *ever* holler at me again I'm gonna shoot you right between the eyes."

Lee squealed like a pig being chased for slaughter.

"Ronny, goddammit," Jamie barked, "why don't you point that gun at me so I can shove it up your ass. Quit fucking around before that thing goes off," he admonished, slapping Tony on the shoulder, pointing towards a white-framed house. Ronny stuffed the revolver into the waistband of his pants.

After a pickup sped by, Tony removed his foot from the brake pedal and the car crept down the road a few hundred feet before turning into a driveway recently paved with a black top.

"Kill the lights," Jamie ordered before exiting the vehicle with Lee and Ronny. They watched Tony reverse the car, his taillights fading into the night like stars diminishing at daybreak.

"I should've shot 'im. I should've shot 'im," Ronny was saying over and over, cursing and kicking his feet against the driveway, watching Tony accelerate like a comet against the darkness. "Why didn't you let me shoot the sonofabitch, Jamie?"

Jamie watched Tony vanish with a sense of longing, beads of sweat forming on his upper lip. "The hell with that fellow. I'm not surprised. Anyway," Jamie spoke as though talking to himself, then nudged Ronny in the ribs, "we might need somebody to take the fall. The hell with him. C'mon."

Ronny aimed a muffled scream at Lee and fired, "Hey. Get your fat ass up here."

Lee broke into a trot, catching up with Jamie and Ronny halfway up the driveway.

Against the Tennessee night fireflies flickered off and on as if sending coded messages, the scent of honeysuckle and roses perfumed the landscape and somewhere a bullfrog was hoarsely trying to clear its throat. The moon hung full, low enough for you to grab a handful and take a bite.

They moved stealthily up to the house that sat isolated from neighbors and noise, a trio of shadows trailing behind like a well-kept secret. Jamie, medium build, the taller of the group, was in the middle, slouched forward with hands buried in his pockets. Curls of brown hair were piled upon his head like a well-groomed hat. Lee was on the left, short, stocky, clean-shaven head reflecting perspiration from the glow of the moon; he had a piercing through both eyebrows. Ronny was the same height as Jamie and equal in weight to Lee, more muscular than flaccid. His blond hair was twisted into a ponytail that hung shoulder length. A diamond stud sparkled from his left earlobe. He had intense deep-set blue eyes that were hard and tacit.

The three walked as though their feet were gloved, smothering sound and significance, until they found themselves abruptly coming to a stop and staring at the front door.

"There's too much damn light out here. Did you know she had floodlights around the house?" Jamie, sweating profusely, turned to Ronny.

Ronny hunched his shoulders. "Never noticed. I guess she leaves 'em on whenever she goes to church. But we ain't gonna be that long anyway."

They stood motionless—Lee with his thumbs hooked into belt loops, Jamie arms folded across his chest and Ronny hands on hips—staring at the front door as if it were an entrance with no exit or an opening that would swallow them whole or a gateway that would lead to places unfamiliar and far away.

"Uh, excuse me," Ronny interrupted the ruminations,

"Are we gonna stand here and whistle 'Dixie' all night or what? Please tell me or what." Jamie and Lee glanced at one another and in unison all three stepped up on the front porch. With his hand made into a fist, Ronny opened the screen door and banged three times, twice in succession. The echo of silence was the only reply. Jamie led and the others followed around to the back where they found a security door, and again Ronny imitated a sledgehammer with the same results. There was a four-door white Chevrolet Caprice parked in the backyard.

"Goddam, it's hot," Lee muttered.

"Shut up and c'mon," Ronny snarled.

They marched single file around the house like actors on a stage under the spotlight of a pale round moon.

"Fatass." Ronny swung open the screen door, making room for Lee.

Lee stamped his feet in anger. "Why you always gotta call me that, Ronny? Just because a fellow's got slow metabolism, you ain't gotta call 'im names."

Ronny spat inches from Lee's sneakers, a ball of phlegm full of hate and contempt. "Get…"

Jamie raised his hand in mid-air, damming words flowing from Ronny's mouth; then cleared a path. "Go ahead, Lee."

With a running start, Lee threw his entire bulk against the door, which cracked and moaned with resistance but refused to yield. With a second and a third effort the door splintered and gave way and Lee found himself stumbling into a darkened room.

"Get out the way." Ronny led them into the living room, turning left and down a hallway. Each footstep forward was counterbalanced with a nervous pause anticipating sound and movement. The paneled walls emitted the call and response of a gospel song on the radio. Lee knocked over a vase sitting on a table and the sound of breaking glass activated an alarm of anguish and fear.

"Who's there? What do you want? Who are you?"

Time was a vacant black hole filled with the rhythmic breathing of the house.

"Uh, good evening ma'am. We're Publishers Clearing House…" Ronny's voice was edged with derision. "I'm Ed McMahon and these two…" He pointed and looked behind him finding only the brand name of two pairs of sneakers in a blur.

Jamie and Lee almost knocked each other down and were in a dead heat running for the door they entered by. They omitted the front porch altogether, leaping through the air and landing with a thud upon the walkway in full stride.

"Hey!" Ronny stood feet inside the front door. Jamie and Lee were huddled together with bewildered faces, glancing from the road to the house. "Where the fuck y'all going? She's just a nigger. She ain't no ghost. Y'all get the fuck back in here!"

Like two puppies with tails between their legs, they diffidently mounted the steps. Inside, an elderly Black woman was on her knees at Ronny's side as if she were an appendage to his body. He had a handful of her gray hair in his hands and she was sobbing quietly.

"Goddam, Ronny!" Jamie's face was grimaced into a scowl. His eyes shifted from the old lady back to Ronny. "What the fuck is she doing here?"

"I guess she lives here," Ronny shot back. "What the fuck were you running for?"

"Is anybody else in the house?" Lee queried.

The woman squirmed and Ronny jerked a handful of hair, lifting her off the floor. "Yeah. The NAACP is having a convention in the other room, asshole."

"Look, Ronny," Jamie admonished, "you were supposed to be casing the house. I thought you said she goes to church on Saturday night. You should've—"

"No. You look, Jamie. You should've cased the house your damn self. And another thing, I'm tired of you trying to tell me what to do all the damn time." He gripped the gun sticking out of his waistband, his countenance radiant with defiance and challenge. "I've had enough of your shit."

Jamie shook his head from side to side with a wan warped smile on his face. "You're full of shit. You know if you pull that gun on me you're gonna have to kill me, don'tcha? 'Cause if you don't, you know I'ma kill you. You think you man enough to pull that gun out of your pants? You man enough to be a man, boy?"

The lady moaned as if she were being crushed by the weight of the tension in the room. Her form was shapeless under the blue loose fitting nightgown. Piles of gray hair were plaited on her head. Her face was brown and worn with wrinkles, sculpted by kisses from her own children as well as those from the neighborhood which had adopted her as "Big Mama." She had dark circles under her eyes that camouflaged a life of youth, beauty, dreams and aging grace. She shifted her gaze upon each of the teenagers standing over her.

"Let's get the money so we can get the ice, man!" Lee

stepped between Jamie and Ronny, inches from Ronny's face. "To hell with this old woman." A half-shadow, half-smile fell over his face. "Methamphetamine."

The word "methamphetamine" flipped a switch in Ronny's head that caused light to gleam through his eyes. It was as if after hours and hours of struggling with a calculus problem, everything suddenly clicked with clarity and resolution. A car advertisement was on the radio and the announcer seemed to talk directly to Jamie, Ronny and Lee.

"Yeah." He looked at Lee as though he'd seen him for the very first time. "Do me a favor, will ya? Get the hell away from me and close the door." He brushed Lee aside with his forearm and yanked the woman to her feet. "Get up, Aunt Jemima." Then to Jamie, "I'ma tie her up, man. Cut that goddam radio off."

Lee ambled into the den, opening a gun rack and inspecting an assortment of weapons, choosing one and sighting imaginary targets. Jamie rambled into a bedroom, grabbing handfuls of diamonds, pearls and rubies and stuffing them into his pockets. He overturned mattresses, closet shelves and dresser drawers. Ronny held the woman down on the bathroom floor, assailing her with a succession of invectives related to her money and her life.

"Oh, God. What did I do to deserve this?" Her voice trod deep, murky waters of hysteria.

"Where's your pocketbook at, bitch?" Ronny screamed, inches away from her face. "Don't make me hit you again."

Jamie stood on the threshold of the bedroom door, listening to Ronny's fist ebb and flow on the woman's face. The ripping of cotton fabric made his flesh crawl.

"Please don't do this," she pleaded, "I've told you

everything." There was a final pulling at the nightgown that sounded like flesh being torn asunder.

"Ronny."

Grunts, moans, cries.

"Ronny?" Jamie's voice, as if he were yelling down a canyon, sounded distant and forlorn, returning hollow in waves of echoes.

Ronny replied between gasps and exertions, "Yo, Jamie. You want some of this?"

"Some of what?"

Lee stomped into the hallway carrying two rifles in his left hand and another in his right. "Somebody's a hunter." He raised the weaponry as though it were a prized deer destined for the taxidermist and searched Jamie's face, finding more questions than answers. "What's going on?"

"This goddammit. This is the only this there is."

Jamie's throat was dry and uncooperative as he tried to force himself to swallow. "Want some, my ass. I got the money, man. Let's get hell out of here."

Lee took a step forward, heavy with guns, hesitancy and curiosity, before being grabbed by Jamie.

"Ronny," Jamie called again. "Ronny?"

"Yeah, yeah, yeah." There was the rustling of clothes being pulled, fastened, straightened. "I'm coming. Hahaha. That's some funny shit. Hahaha."

He stood before the bathroom mirror running a wet comb through his blond hair. "Hey...Jamie, you got the money?"

"C'mon, Ronny. Yeah, I got the money."

"Where's fatass?"

"He's right here. Let's move goddamit!"

"Fatass? You ever had a blow job? C'mere, man. Won't have to use your hand so much."

The idea caused the wheels of thought to spin with such velocity that they threaten to derail Lee's brain, caused his lips to form words without sound.

"Ronny," Jamie's voiced boomed down the corridor, "leave that old woman alone and get out here. Either get out here or I'm coming to get you."

Ronny had the revolver tucked under his armpit and was turned sideways looking back into the mirror, impersonating Robert De Niro in a scene from *Taxi Driver* —you talking to me? "Go hot-wire the car in the backyard, Jamie, and then when you get through go to hell, willya?"

"I don't need to hot-wire anything," Jamie shot back. "I got the keys, asshole."

Ronny stomped to the bathroom door, peeped into the hallway. "You got the what? Why in hell didn't you say so? And who you calling asshole asshole?" He leaned against the doorjamb, the pistol pointed toward the ceiling. He looked at Lee looking at him. "Boy, are you ever gonna get any pussy?" Then back to Jamie. "Look, man. Pull the car around. I'm gonna find something to tie this bitch up with. I'll meet y'all out front. Is that OK with you?"

"Fuck you."

"Sounds good."

Jamie and Lee unbolted and escaped through the back door, loaded the trunk of the four-door Caprice Classic with the spoils of invasion and pulled the sedan around front, engine humming. Jamie slid from behind the wheel. "Let me go get this motherfucker. I'll be right back." Lee punched the scan button until an alternative rock station zeroed in.

With the force of a tornado, Jamie re-entered the house intent upon dragging Ronny out by his lapels either consciously or unconsciously. Either way didn't matter. But halfway down the hallway, waves of nausea began to rise from the deepest part of his guts. Chills swept over him as if in the initial phases of pneumonia. His body staggered from the report of the second gunshot. He rushed to the bathroom, where Ronny stood over the partially nude elderly Black woman, smoke wafting from the blue barrel of the gun. Their eyes met, Jamie's full of disgust, Ronny's indifferent.

"I tied her up, Jamie."

"Ronny," Jamie held his head between both hands, "what are you doing, man?"

Ronny stepped inches from Jamie's face, their noses almost touching. "Do I need to shoot her again? Am I man enough now, Jamie?" He shoved the gun into his pocket and brushed past Jamie out of the front door.

Jamie stood in the bathroom, hand over his mouth, fighting the urge to throw up, watching blood drool from the corner of the woman's mouth. He hit the light switch on the wall, ran out of the house, leaving the front door open, jumped behind the wheel and rocketed into open country spaces, smashing mailboxes and anything else that got between him and the road to anywhere.

Walter Robinson didn't have to wait for his alarm clock to shatter into shrill screams, his wife to nudge him awake or for a sunrise to peel back the covers of night. He met the morning with eyes wide open. It had been a long night and a short morning. His time was divided between the squad room and the emergency room. He had showered, slipped into pajama pants and between the covers, flat on his back, hands clasped behind his head. It was three in the morning. His thoughts had wandered between praying that she would be alright and killing the bastards that did this to his grandmother. He remembered distinctly summer afternoons on Big Mama and Grandaddy's farm, the only home he'd known since age twelve, when both his parents were killed in an accident outside of Memphis. It was wonderful when he moved to the country to escape the noise, concrete and dirt of urban decay of his old neighborhood and enter into the clean air, cooler temps and people walking gravel roads that were the essence of rural living. Seemed liked blue skies prevailed and the sun was always shining someplace even when neither was. What Walter remembered most about growing up in the country were the colors and smells of wide open spaces. The green fields of cabbage, collards; the yellow shoots of corn, squash; melons, tomatoes heavy with ripeness; the hoarse brownness of a dog's bark and the groveling of condemned hogs. And then there was the rain that had a way of anointing all these smells, including yours, like praises going up from a Sunday morning congregation, cleansing, sanctifying, liberating, reconciling man with himself, the earth and the God of this universe.

He rubbed his wife's shoulder, shifted his weight in one deft motion and was out of bed, sliding his feet into a pair of slippers. She murmured unintelligible words, filling the void that his leaving created. Sleep was elusive as a handful of water when, an hour later, Walter found himself on the couch, staring into the blankness of pre-dawn. Inundated with waves of silence, a sense of helplessness began to close in upon him like the paneled walls of the room he occupied. He paced from den to kitchen on automatic pilot, creating a well-worn path the distance thereof, before collapsing like an airplane with engines sputtering, fading.

Face downward, eyes closed, he wanted to cry but found only bitterness and frustration buried within the folds of the couch. His wife whispered his name and he rolled over, blinking fiercely as if she were an apparition. She rubbed his shoulders, her touch feeling foreign to him as a mistress or a new lover.

"Big Mama wouldn't hurt a fly, Sherry. She's never turned anyone down for anything. This is so unnecessary. Now I feel unnecessary. I even feel out of place at work."

"You'll only get in the way down at that station. You need to stay home today," she replied.

"And do what? It's even worse around here. At least at work I can pretend that I know what the hell I'm doing."

That hurt. But the truth usually does, as Sherry dropped her arms helplessly by her side. Lately the marriage had gone from bad to worse and the both of them were doing a lot of faking, she probably more so than Walter. She was tired of faking that she liked going to the same places he went to, tired of faking interest in police work over breaking bread and conversation, tired of faking how wonderful lovemaking was when it was routine as an antiquated dance step: one, two, three, kick. She wanted to wrap her arms about Walter Robinson's neck and hold on tight as though he were a lifeguard rescuing her from suffocating waters, but she would only be exploring uncharted waters of faking. But Sherry loved Big Mama just as much as he did, that she could not fake, and it hurt her to see him in this condition. With daylight rising from the ashes of night, Sherry pressed her lips to his and Walter ran his fingers through her black, freshly washed hair, which could have been a childhood memory, fragrant, visible and alive with remembrance.

At 7 a.m. the drive to work was already hot, sticky, and miserable. The air conditioner in Walter Robinson's car had given up the ghost long ago and it made precious little sense to spend money he didn't have on a 1988 Chrysler to get it fixed when the four-eighty air cooling system was just as effective and a helluva lot cheaper: four windows down and eighty miles an hour. The city seemed to be smoldering; the streets, buildings, people all looked haggard and irritated. Forrest, Tennessee, not unlike most American municipalities, was two cities, separate and unequal. Economic prosperity had come to the town of 60,000 and the white population followed the money trail northward into the suburbs, while the predominantly Black east side felt the draft of white flight in the form of higher unemployment, crime rates and just plain apathy. And like most Southern cities, below the surface racial tensions permeated every aspect of small-town life. From school boards to county commissions, from police brutality to school desegregation to city hall, sins of the past were like a cancer that demanded extrication but instead was covered with Band-Aids to hide the festering, egregious wound. No matter how many attempted cover-ups, the odor was always a reminder of just how deep and diseased the hurt had become. This morning was more pungent than most.

Walter loosened his tie, tuned in the local talk radio station and merged aggressively onto the bypass. It was all over the local news. About his grandmother being attacked, sodomized. News reports called it vicious. Incomprehensible. Shameful. And no suspects appre-hended. Callers voiced outrage. Demanded a return to days of law and order. Public executions and castrations. He snapped the radio off, driving in silence to the engine's own peculiar rhythm. All of that talk was only squeezing the thoughts already barricading the clarity of his reasoning. This wasn't just an incident in New York or some newsflash at the top of the hour. This was his life, and it felt like he was having an out-of-body experience, something real and not real simultaneously. He suspected that it was front-page news in the local paper, and that was one of the reasons he had left the paper lying in the front yard. He would find out all he needed to know in the squad room.

He adjusted his rearview mirror, beads of sweat surfacing upon his forehead, giving his ebony skin a smooth sheen. What were the city planners thinking, putting stop lights on a goddam bypass? Why in hell didn't they just lay down speed bumps instead? Every other day somebody got mangled or killed on this concrete loop. He slammed the horn with the side of his fist, jammed his foot onto the accelerator, and cut across two lanes of traffic, feeling two tons of steel lurch beneath him, gaining speed.

It was better, Walter reasoned, to always remember

someone you loved in the prime of their vim and vigor. That was not his grandmother lying in a hospital bed with tubes and hoses running through her veins but someone who had snatched her body. His grandmother always had warm words flowing from her mouth, arms wide as a hug and a smile that never condemned, even when he was in the wrong. Just the way a grandmother should be. He probably should have stopped by the hospital on his way to work to check on her. But what good was that when she was in a coma? It would only serve to anger or depress him or a combination of the two. Besides, Sherry said she would take care of that. And if anything, maybe this whole incident would bring him and his wife closer, instead of their being pulled apart by constant bickering over trivial episodes.

The past few hours had been as surreal as a Salvador Dalí painting, just like the yellow caution signal swinging fifty yards away. He could slam on the brakes now and come to a screeching stop beneath the light or he could floor the gas pedal and streak through it like a comet, maybe. Either way, it made little difference. With the way things had been going lately and the turn his life had taken recently, those weren't bad odds. The only drawback would be he might contribute to someone else being maimed or dying, and that was becoming old as moldy bread. After all, it was from others dying that he made his living.

Walter Robinson stomped the gas pedal against the floor and wasn't sure if all four wheels of the Chrysler were still on the ground, his vehicle speeding like an aircraft approaching takeoff. Five yards away, the light blinked red but he barely noticed, hurtling through time and space as if he were trying to break the bonds of gravity. He pulled a pack of smokes from his breast pocket, dragged one free with his teeth and lit it in one motion. Within minutes there would be other traffic signals, then the congestion of the downtown commuters, finally the Fourth Precinct.

After swerving into the parking lot, Walter adjusted his necktie and grabbed his gun and badge from the glove compartment. He squashed the remainder of the cigarette underfoot and took the steps two at a time, bounding into the squad room as if he had springs on his feet.

"Robinson! What the hell are you doing here?" Lieutenant Peters was a big, broad-shouldered white man with an authoritative mien that he wore like a well-tailored suit.

"Talk to me, Pete." Walter's face was contorted into a question mark.

"Right now there ain't nothing to say." Lieutenant Peters looked around the squad room, noticed that he and Walter had become the center of attention, as if they were on a slide under a microscope. "Still chasing down leads." His voice dropped an octave. "You're supposed to be off today."

Walter shook his head. "You gotta put me on this case, Pete."

"No. Hell, no. You're too close, Walt. Your judgment'll get burned. Not only that," Lieutenant Peters signed some papers handed to him by his secretary—an auburn-haired woman with short cropped hair in her early forties—then looked up again, "you're Homicide. And your grandmother is still living, right? Right, Walter?"

Walter shrugged. "If you wanna call it that, Pete. It's all tubes and machines now."

The secretary thanked her boss and parted with a

sympathetic smile towards Walter.

"Well," Lieutenant Peters shrugged back, "you never know. Your grandmother is a strong woman. But if you choose to stay in this squad room, Homicide is that way." He pointed to a cubicled area of the squad room. "Your partner has been asking 'bout you all morning."

"C'mon, Pete. Violent crimes, homicide, it's all the same goddam thing!"

"Not for you it ain't."

Walter threw his hands up, turned in the direction of his desk.

"Walt," Lieutenant Peters barked. "They left finger-prints all over the place. Lab should have some results soon. And every cop in the country is looking for your grandmother's car. I'll keep you posted soon as I hear something." He opened his office door and closed it shut on the "thank you" Walter offered in response.

The squad room hummed from an air unit that worked half the time and the whir of fans at full speed. The homicide unit was small, oftentimes found itself overworked if there was a flurry of murderous intent and sometimes doubled as Violent Crime: rape, assault, hit-and-runs. Walter got an array of head tosses, hellos and handshakes as he made his way to his desk. There were no looks of sympathy and no one mentioned the ordeal; it was another day at the office and business as usual. And as usual there was a mound of paperwork stacked upon his desk, always paperwork. Closed cases, cases in progress, unsolved cases. A tall, lanky officer in a short-sleeved shirt and red tie with rings of perspiration under his arms sat opposite the desk of Walter. His eyes were pools of deep blue, his blond hair resting on his forehead partly due to sweat and partly to fashion. Joseph Hardegree, Vanderbilt grad, stood to greet his partner of two years with a pat on the back.

"I've tried to call you, Walt. Thought you were taking some time off."

Walter shuffled some papers around his desk. "Nah. I've had all of those walls I can stand. A man needs to work." He looked as though he were awaiting an answer.

"Your timing is impeccable," replied Detective Hardegree, slipping into a blue sports coat. "Just found a body in a field on the northeast side."

"Good. I'll drive."

The victim, a Black female around thirty years old, had been dead for approximately twenty-four hours with an odor of decomposition in the initial stages. She was found by two teenagers with fishing poles on their way to a nearby pond. They reminded Walter of himself on his grandparents' farm when he was a barefoot kid in overalls, going fishing. How sunrise caught him eating a hurried breakfast of hen eggs and juice before grabbing his cane pole and empty coffee can, slamming the wooden screen door behind him, scurrying off the front porch to meet Eddie Woods to capture fresh bait wriggling from the richness of black earth, destined for martyrdom in the kingdom of catfish. The day spilled over the borders of time and between swimming, gathering blackberries and stringing fish, twilight tiptoed up on them like a cat burglar in search of jewels, the foreign language of crickets echoing among the hills. And like salmon during the spawning season, their feet found their own paths home, interspersed with rock throwing and wrestling matches.

"Walt."

Yes. This part of the county was not unlike the part where he had spent the summers of his youth. The same flat land full of corn, cotton, soybeans. The country people with calloused hands scuffling to eke a living from the land they loved, whom the land did not always love in return, but who nevertheless remained generous and thankful for something as simple as rain. He remembered the way freedom caressed his face as he sat astride the majestic power of his grandfather's horse, he being the Lone Ranger looking for Tonto and the nearest sunset.

"Walt!"

"Hey!"

Detective Hardegree motioned, waited for Walter to look his way. "Over here."

They both ducked beneath yellow police tape, stood over the body, hands in latex gloves, pencils scratching on notepads. Walter kneeled closer to the body. She was of medium complexion, had shoulder-length braids, a blue denim blouse, and beige slacks. Through her ripped blouse, the name Lucas could be seen tattooed over her right breast. There was a diamond ring on her left hand, a gold bracelet on her right wrist and no identification on the body.

"She was definitely stabbed, Joe," commented Walter, "but where's the blood?"

Detective Hardegree squatted beside his partner. "I was

gonna ask you the same thing. So she had to have been killed and dumped here, right?"

Walter surveyed the landscape around him. "Maybe. Maybe not. Judging by all the jewelry she's wearing, the perp didn't have nothing but killing on his mind." They stood, Walter putting away his pad and pencil, Detective Hardegree reaching into his back pocket and wiping his brow with a handkerchief. "Let's let the ME decide. Why don't you ask the neighbors that way if they heard anything and I'll take the other direction?"

"Wait a minute, Walt." Detective Hardegree stuffed the handkerchief back into his pocket. "I'm the primary here. I took the call, remember?"

Walter nodded in apology. "You're right. But I need this one, Joe." His words were clear with sincerity, heavy as a plea.

Detective Hardegree squinted in the direction of a home of potential witnesses, its roof shimmering from heat and glare, before turning back to his partner. "No problem. I got enough shit in red under my name anyway. But look, before we start talking to neighbors let's go over the crime scene one more time with the CSI. I still say she was killed somewhere else and dumped here."

Thirty minutes later Detective Hardegree gave a yell that echoed in waves across the field. He raised a baseball cap on the end a of stick as though it were the flag of a conqueror hoisted after overrunning enemy territory. All evidence from the crime scene was bagged, a photographer snapped various pictures from various angles, a chalk outline was drawn around the body, two attendants rolled the corpse into the rear of an ambulance headed for the morgue, and a reporter wanted comments from Walter, who informed her without breaking stride that no details were available as of yet as he balled the latex gloves into his rear pocket and slid behind the wheel of an unmarked police car. His partner waved off any further questions.

"Whew," exclaimed Joe Hardegree, entering the vehicle, "hot as hell, huh?" Both men buckled up.

Walter Robinson was rubbing his eyes, trying to remove fatigue and redness. He released a sigh as heavy as a final breath. He rolled up the window and flipped the AC on high.

"You look tired, Walt," noted Joe, genuinely concerned.

"Man," Walter said, checking his side-view mirror, turning the vehicle around, "you're always on the J-O-B." He recognized the direction of the conversation quickly changing its course. "What'd you do this weekend?"

Joe ran his fingers through his hair. "Ahhh, yard work on Saturday, church on Sunday." He dropped the visor, wiped more sweat from his brow in the mirror.

"Damn. I thought I had an exciting forty-eight hours. What did the preacher preach about?"

"Forgiveness."

Walter's eyes became lasers boring into the side of Joe's head. "You a fucking comedian now, Joe?"

"What? You asked me what he preached about. That's what he preached about, Walt."

"If anybody needs forgiveness it's some of these goddam preachers. It's either money, Mercedes or sex. Most of the time, same sex." There were tones of satisfaction in Walter's declaration.

"Look, don't start that crap again, here. Just because

you had a bad experience with a preacher or two, you can't generalize like that, Walt. C'mon, you a cop, of all people."

"I'm gonna generalize and tell you what I think about cops one of these days too. But as far as preachers go, it's not just preachers. It's the churches they operate too." Walter slid on a pair of Wayfarer sunglasses. "Alright, you're a Methodist, right? OK. What makes the Methodists better than the Baptists or the Baptists better than the Catholics or the Catholics better than the Holy Rollers?"

"Who says one group is better than the other? What do you mean, better than the other?"

"Well hell, Joe. The Methodists say you gotta do it this way to see God, the Baptists say you need to go under the water, the Holy Rollers ain't having none of that and the Catholics swear they are on a first-name basis with God. They call him the Pope. And not only that, half the sonofabitches in church are the biggest liars, thieves, whores, whoremongers you'll find anywhere. Hell, it's hard to tell the difference between saints and sinners any more. Matter of fact, I trust some of the guys we've busted over the years more than I do some of these dressed-up, perfumed, church-going bastards."

"Let me ask you something, Walt." Joe turned in his seat. "You remember the guys that Vice busted last month? The counterfeiters? That was a big-time operation and those guys printed a lot of funny money, high-quality funny money at that. So my question is this. Why didn't you when you cashed your check burn the money or give it away?"

Walter's face was a blank page scrawled with bewilderment. He focused his eyes back upon the road. "And the price of tea in China is still…or is this your brain on drugs?"

"What I'm trying to say, Detective, is that just because you've had a couple of bad experiences with a church doesn't mean that you can condemn all of them any more than you stop spending money because a few bills turned up counterfeit." He swallowed, gathering steam to continue his point. "Just like some doctors are quacks, but..."

"OK, OK, Joe. I got you." Walt turned the vehicle onto Ridgemont Avenue. "But we're not talking about finances or physicians. Or one church, for that matter. I guess I'm getting at organized religion period. You know how many wars have been waged in the name of religion? It's all bullshit if you ask me. The Muslims get upset and will declare 'jihad' over every little thing in the name of God, the Jews, if you let them tell it, are special in the eyes of God, and Christians, if you don't believe in Jesus you're already destined for hell. That's one thing the Baptists, Methodists and Catholics agree on. Now, I didn't even mention Buddhists and Hindus."

Joe chuckled. "Well, goddam, Walt, I'm glad you gave somebody a break. You just insulted most of the people in the known world." He laughed again, trying to lighten the mood, then became serious. "So, you don't believe in God any more, is that what you're trying to tell me?"

"Now that's funny. I'm trying to tell you that it's religion I don't believe in any more. God ain't got nothing to do with it. Matter of fact, I think God done got out of the religion business. You talking about a counterfeit ring, religion is probably the biggest racket going today. In a way it's worse than the best narcotic."

Joe shook his head from side to side. "Wow. How did we

become so cynical? But what you're failing to consider in your philosophy of cynicism is that organized religion allows one to get to God, Walt. I mean, it's sorta...sorta like a blue-print," Joe's ten fingers became vowels, consonants, his hands uttering tongues of their own. "Your faith, whatever you choose, merely sets parameters and guidelines for wor-shiping the God of your choosing. What you do when you get there is another thing. But no, Walt. Without religion, man would be lost. Christianity is the cornerstone of our country."

"So is slavery," quipped Walter from the corner of his mouth, coming to a four-way stop, turning the unmarked squad car onto Preston, accelerating.

"Don't start that shit again, Walt."

"I mean, can you imagine a group of people taking the Bible and justifying their wickedness and telling another group of people, 'Servants, obey your masters'?" He paused. "What shit?"

"Race shit. Besides, whoever said the slaves believed that anyway?"

"Amen, brother! But Joe, you can't separate religion shit from race shit. Hell, there ain't too much shit you can separate from religion. Religion is the large intestine of all fecal matter." He nudged his partner in the ribs. "How's that for philosophy and cynicism?"

"Speaking of shit..."

"Yeah, you're right. Corny shit at that."

Exasperated, Joe said, "So what's the answer according to Walt Robinson?"

"I feel that you need to find God the best way you can by any methods available and the hell with doing it the way some people tell you is the way it ought to be done and they ain't doing it themselves."

"Well, see, you just started a religion, Walt. Sooner or later somebody's gonna be attracted to the way you're doing it, will want to do it your way and that'll spark a movement of...Walterians, yeah...that'll be the name of the new religion, Walterians—and hell, somebody will put you in the category with the Christians, Buddhists and good ole Methodists, of which I happen to be one, and criticize the hell out of you."

"Where is this conversation going, Joe?"

"Right past salvation and straight to heaven, brother. With you leading the way, of course." He slapped Walter Robinson on the shoulder.

"You mind if I smoke?"

Joe Hardegree grinned like a man with a newly acquired advantage. "Not at all. I'm your partner, Walt."

"You little no-good bastard! What in hell have you done? Answer me, goddammit!"

June McAlister slapped her youngest son across the face with such ferocity that she thought she had broken her right hand. Ronny didn't flinch, but stayed rooted to the middle of the living-room floor, wiping away blood from the corner of his mouth.

"And then you have the nerve to run back here," she continued. "The lies I had to tell the police to try and cover your little butt. The cops are not that dumb. They knew I was holding out on 'em. But you've been stupid all of your life, you know that? Of all the places, why would you come back here? The cops'll probably bust down the door any minute now. You're just like your father. No good and stupid."

Ronny's eyes were defiant and his face felt as if it were afire. "I never knew my father. Can you tell me something about my father, Mama?"

"Hell, no. You should be happy you didn't know him. Who in hell would want to know that asshole? I haven't received a child support payment from that sonofabitch in ten years. At the rate you're going, you're going to be a bigger loser than he ever was." She put her hands on her hips. "Why couldn't you be like your brother, Tony? He's going to vocation school to make something out of himself. I'm so thankful that you two don't have the same daddy."

Ronny exploded, "I can't be nobody but me. What made me so hard to love, Mama?"

She shook her finger inches from his face. "Why, you miserable little wretch. I've feed, housed and clothed you and tried to give you everything you needed all your life the best I knew how. Why wasn't that good enough for you? Now look at you. You come in here dirty, hungry, with the cops crawling all over the place, and got the nerve to talk to me about love? You've been nothing but trouble with a capital T every since you started to walk. Killing neighborhood animals, skipping school, stealing cars, reform school. You know how many nights I've stayed awake worrying about you? I worried so much I just gave up and wished you wouldn't come home at all. And how I had to put up with the neighbors whispering behind my back about you. I only admitted to being your mama when I absolutely had to. Love? You got it all backwards, sonny. I should be asking you why you never loved me."

"You wouldn't let me," Ronny fired back, "even when I tried to you compared that to Tony's. You think Tony's so innocent and pure. Like he's never done anything wrong. He's in just as much trouble as I'm in. It's not my fault my daddy ran out on you when I was born. Maybe you oughta blame him instead of me. Or better yet, maybe you oughta blame yourself, Mama. Or maybe everything you hate about me is the same thing you see every time you look in the mirror."

June McAlister pulled back her arm and let the palm of her right hand land squarely on Ronny's jaw creating a hollow, flat echo. "What do you mean he's in as much trouble as you? You can't drag him into your mess this time. I've already taken him to the police and cleared his name. So you can forget that pipe dream. You little bastard. Why don't you blame the fall of Adam and Eve on me too, willya? I'm not your mother. Not after what you've done. The cops told me all about it. Don't you know I'm going to be an old woman one day? What you did to that old Black woman, you did to me. At first I didn't want to believe 'em, but now," she tried to peer deeply into his eyes, "yeah. I believe every word."

Ronny used his tongue as a spelunker, exploring the damage to the inside of his cheek; his eyes were following the trail of a cockroach making its way across the linoleum floor.

"It was you. It had to be you," she continued. "My Tony wouldn't do nothing like that. I guess my wish came true. It'll be a long goddam time before you ever come home again, you little bastard. They're gonna lock you up for a long time, and if that woman dies, so will you. And I'm gonna help 'em. If it comes down between Tony and you, by God, I'll help 'em."

June McAlister turned her back on her son, grabbed a pot from the dish rack, filled it with water, and set it atop high heat from an electric range.

"Mama."

"Get outa my house!"

"Mama?"

"Get out my sight!"

"Don't you ever hit me again, you hear?"

She turned around, charged towards Ronny, hand over her head as if it were a sword seeking separation of bone and flesh.

Ronny met her in full stride, grabbed her around the neck and shoved her against the kitchen sink. Her throat palpitating in his hands felt like the supple body of the gray pigeon he'd held once when he was ten years old before smashing it in the head with a baseball bat. He stared through her, oblivious to the gurgling noises emanating from her throat, the blue eyes bulging with red veins and the purpleness of her complexion growing in proportion to the increased intensity of his strength. For the second time in less than twenty-four hours he held the power of life and death in his hands. It was the reality of her nails digging into the flesh of his grip that hit him like a sudden jolt interrupting a daydream. He tossed her to the floor in a crumpled heap of coughs and blood, opened the refrigerator, grabbing a handful of cold fried chicken, and walked out of the kitchen, out of the house.

Big Mama.

Sherry Robinson stood beside the hospital bed of her husband's grandmother and whispered the words "Big Mama" as if they were a prayer. Big Mama had been her grandmother every since she and Walter began dating all those years ago. More so, she had come to know and love Dissie Marshall with the affection of a biological daughter. Big Mama was the pillar of the Robinson clan whom one could lean upon for support or to glean words of encouragement from her many fields of wisdom. How to make a certain casserole, what flowers would survive the winter, homemade remedies for common aches and pains? Big Mama was just a phone call away. Sherry's love for Big Mama was surpassed only by her admiration for her. Talk about independent! Big Mama would call it independence; Sherry knew it as just plain old stubbornness. Never missed a Sunday or Wednesday night of church or any night the doors of the church were opened, no matter how poorly she felt. Always found something to do in her yard, whether it was pulling weeds from the garden or raking leaves (swore it keep her bones from stiffening worse than they already were)—her garden being the envy of the entire community. Big Mama's knowledge about horticulture surpassed that of a lot of PhDs. She could tell you not only the name of any flower but how to nurture it to its maximum potential. And imagine still driving herself to the store and anywhere else she wanted to go for that matter at seventy-eight years old. It seemed that everyone in the Beech Springs community knew and loved Big Mama. How could anybody do such a horrible thing? At one time or another, she had to have fed the entire neighborhood. Her home was considered a safe haven for the entire community. It would be a rare occasion when Sherry and Walter visited every Sunday that they would not find some neighbor there who had stopped by just to say hello. Sherry delighted in teasing Big Mama about the potential beaus paying their respects to her. She would quip, "Honey, used to be these old men couldn't do nothing but look, maybe pet it now and then. But with all this Viagra mess, it's a whole new ball game. Don't really matter to me. I hung up my cleats a long time ago, chile. I can spot a horny old man a mile away." They both would double over with laughter, Big Mama tapping Sherry lightly on the shoulder.

Intensive care visits were limited to two hours. Sherry glanced at her watch. She squeezed Big Mama's hand with her own, leaned forward just inches from her ear. "I love you." She leaned closer still, kissing Big Mama on her forehead, repeating herself. Then Sherry felt a slight pressure around her hand, like a faint signal from a distant radio station trying to tune in. She watched Big Mama perform a succession of rapid eye movements and responded, "I know. I love you too."

She kissed Big Mama again, walked out of intensive care, wiping tears from her eyes, pulled a cell phone from her purse and tried to control her hand from shaking long enough to push one button.

This was the part of the job Walter hated most.

The victim was twenty-nine-year-old Telissa Williamson. The medical examiner had concluded that she had been stabbed eight times and had not been moved from another location; the stab wounds had been so deep that most of her bleeding was internal, resulting in very little blood at the scene of the crime. Walter enjoyed the natural high that came with the collecting of evidence, sewing it together with a single thread of logic, interrogating suspects in a room they called "the tomb," applying psychological pressure—he likened it to two people driving autos at a hundred miles per hour towards each other on a one-lane road—until either he baled out or the suspect broke down in confession. Intellect and reason. That's what separated homicide detectives from other cops. He could never see himself behind a desk once more or walking a beat ever again. He'd paid his dues, was still paying them. Homicide was where the adrenalin rush was to be found, each day needing a little more to surpass the day before, feeling anxious when not trying to solve a killing, like a junkie who never knows the definition of addiction. Getting into the mind of killers. Anticipating their next thought, word, deed. Some days the perpetrators practically walked through the front door; and to this day some murders are unsolved. Therefore, with homicide detectives, it was either caviar or crumbs. Reality only came in one color: black and white. Walter Robinson considered himself beholden only to the Truth. The means of attaining that lofty ideal oftentimes became tainted, smeared, dirtied, but the basic integrity of the Truth prevailed. The names on the board under his name were all in black except two, which gave testament to the expertise of his skills. He considered himself a high priest for Justice and took every sin that evoked the Sixth Commandment personally. Being murder police meant that he spoke for the victims who had their voices silenced, told their stories for them, stood in the gap for the sake of righteousness. And being murder police was also as close to playing God as he'd ever get.

There was a flight of stairs leading to a brick house with a porch light on. In the dusk the light shimmered with a wavering glow. The yard was neatly kept and there was a yellow Honda parked in the driveway. Near by a dog alerted the neighborhood to the presence of strangers. Detectives Walter Robinson and Joe Hardegree rang the bell to 1536 Lancaster, waited, then pushed the buzzer a second time while checking the environment around them. A light sprang on in the living room and a young slender woman in her mid-twenties with a towel tied around her head came to the door in a blue flannel blouse and white slacks. The detectives identified themselves and for the sake of formality asked if she was Rosetta Williamson. The girl shook her head and called for her mother without taking her eyes off the officers.

"Yes? Yes, I'm Rosetta Williamson." Rosetta Williamson was drying her hands on her apron upon her approach. Standing beside her daughter, they could have passed for twins in appearance and youthfulness, Rosetta with big brown eyes and dimples in both cheeks.

Walter introduced himself and his partner and they both presented their badges.

"Homicide. Homicide?" Mrs Williamson's hand covered her mouth as if it were an automatic reflex. "Why are you here?" Her eyes flashed from Walter to Detective Hardegree. "What do you want with me?"

"I think you better sit down, Mrs Williamson." Detective

Hardegree put his hand on her elbow, trying to guide her to a nearby seat.

She shook him off violently. "No. I want you to tell me why you're here." Her youngest daughter moved behind her mother.

"Do you know Telissa Annette Williamson? I'm sorry, ma'am. Your daughter was found deceased earlier this morning. We need—"

"'Lissa? Oh God, oh my God!"

Mrs Williamson stumbled backwards into the embrace of her other child, their sobs and moans merging, becoming cries like the sound of hair being pulled from a human scalp.

"Ma'am. We need you to come down to identify…" Walter broke his words in half and turned to his partner, who was staring out of a window as if the approaching night would bring with it compassion and comprehension.

Every few seconds Jamie Mansfield checked over his shoulder, looked left and right, and tried to look as inconspicuous as possible. He wore round black shades in the fashion of John Lennon, had dyed his brown hair blond and stooped his shoulders in an effort to reduce his height. Trying to become as insipid as the beige paint on the walls was his objective. It seemed as though he'd been standing in line for ever to buy a ticket. One-way. There were two Spanish-speaking people ahead of him, one an elderly white woman at the ticket window who was having a hard time with the sending and/or receiving of information vital to her destination. She proceeded to pull out a bag full of coins, much to the chagrin of the attendant and a line of potential customers.

Jamie checked his surroundings for about the twenty-sixth time. The bus station was dirty and unkempt. Papers were strewn, wastebaskets unemptied, empty soda cans tossed about. And the aroma of urine from the direction of the bathroom was like a blast of hot air from a basement furnace. Overall, the place had the stickiness of filth. Jamie had heard that a Greyhound bus was nothing but a poor man's airplane and now he couldn't agree more.

He shook his head and wondered how it all went wrong. It seemed like years ago. They were just supposed to rob the joint and get the hell out of there. Rape and murder wasn't the way they drew up the plans. That goddam psychotic, Ronny. Jamie was surprised that he hadn't killed somebody before now, or that somebody hadn't smoked his little ass. It was either that or jail. Ever since grade school, Ronny had wanted to be a badass, as though he were trying to get even with the world in general or everyone else in particular. All they had to do was get the money and go. But Jamie couldn't blame it all on Ronny, shouldn't blame him for any of it. First, Ronny had been a friend, no matter how bad he acted, and he knew that at one time Ronny would cut off his right arm for him if he ask for it. He admired the sonofabitch for his raw courage and brute strength: but now, after the fight last night, he doubt if they would ever speak to one another again. Secondly, he, Jamie, was supposed to be in charge of the operation. He conceived it, planned it after Ronny cased the joint and led it, not Ronny. Hell, if he was any kind of a leader, he thought to himself, he should've gone into that bathroom and yank Ronny the hell up outa there. And what kind of leader would plan some shit without having a solid getaway plan? He didn't know where the other guys were. All he knew was that Lee still had the guns and was supposed to be laying low and Ronny was supposed to have the car and could be God knows anywhere, and here he was, the leader, standing in line at a Greyhound bus station ready to take a ten-hour ride to Cincinnati, trying to blend with a bunch of Hispanics, poor Blacks, old crippled folks and of course white trash.

Through the window, Jamie saw a patrol car pull into the bus station parking lot. He could feel the perspiration begin to roll down his armpits. He tried to swallow but nearly gagged from the cotton that seemed to fill his mouth. Before, the station was filled with the clamor of conversations, CD players and the shrill laughter of children; now there was nothing but the pounding of his own heart.

His first impulse was flight. But with the bus station in the heart of downtown, escape would be short lived. And when the other guys had mace, batons and .40-caliber weapons the odds didn't favor fighting. Jamie pulled off his shades and slid them into his breast pocket. He took a deep breath, prolonged its release and began role-playing; he'd been told he favored Matt Damon.

Two white officers entered the premises. Jamie acknowledged their presence with eye contact, brief and indifferent, and nodded in their direction. The more slender of the two officers headed for the administrative offices and shook hands with the manager who closed the door behind them. The other cop was a big redhead with a crew cut and a military gait, who, judging by his physique, was an ex-jock or former soldier in Sam's army. He sauntered over to the waiting area, where three Black guys were lounging in chairs and articulating loudly with intense gesticulations. Jamie, turning his upper torso, couldn't hear what was being said, only that the Black guys were simmering with hate, standing and reaching into their pockets for ID. Jamie turned around, moved forward in line, covered his mouth with his hand to camouflage laughter. As long as there were Black people in the world, he thought, white folks would always get away with crime. Its one of the things that makes America a great country. Here he was, a robber, thief, accessory to rape and murder and a white boy who could've had a suitcase full of dynamite, and nobody suspected him of a goddam thing. He remembered a few years ago when he talked some Black kids into meeting him at the mall. He was to enter Cat's record store first and then the two Black kids would come in afterwards. Boy, did he rack up that day! The store security was so busy following the Black kids around that he went practically unnoticed. But the Black guys got sore as hell when they all met to divide the goods. They wanted to know why he didn't boost Snoop Dogg or 50 Cent. Jamie tried to give them a Nirvana CD but ended up settling the affair with cash instead.

The slender cop emerged from the office with the manager standing in the doorway. He joined his partner in the interrogation of the Greyhound three and, satisfied with the outcome, harassed them no more. The big cop roused a drunk from his sleep and they gave the place a final once-over before the both of them exited the premises, looking to make the world safe from stragglers, loiterers and just plain old hangers-on.

Jamie put his dark glasses back on and thought that he would make a damn good actor, if he ever was spotted sitting in a goddam soda fountain. The person ahead of him collected his ticket and change and stepped aside. Jamie moved forward and laid cash on the counter, knowing that in less than half a day he would be on the banks of the Ohio river. Thank God.

According to Rosetta Williamson, Lucas, the name tattooed on her daughter's breast, came with a last name as well, Witherspoon. She confirmed what the detectives suspected, that the two were intimately involved, and that she knew the young man well. Mrs Williamson agreed to cooperate any way possible with Detectives Robinson and Hardegree, allowing them entrance to her daughter's apartment, which was on the second floor of a newly constructed townhouse. Inside, it was tastefully decorated with the latest in contemporary furniture, live plants, family photos and artistic prints. There were large windows, which allowed the sun to inundate the apartment with waves of light.

Detective Hardegree started in the den, Walter scoured the back of the apartment. Her bedroom suite was carved from cherry wood, carpet thick as Bermuda grass, sensually perfumed and powdered. Her closet was lined with the neatness of a perfectionist. On the dresser lay a Brighton watch, a beeper and a closed jewelry box. On the bedside table, like a faithful lover, was a diary with an ink pen for a bookmarker. Walter thumbed the pages of the diary and bagged it and the beeper before leaving the bedroom.

"Walter," Detective Hardegree greeted him with a smile and a framed eight-by-ten-inch photo in his right hand, "meet Lucas Witherspoon."

Back in the squad room the first thing Detectives Robinson and Hardegree did was to make a beeline for Lieutenant Peters' office.

"Sit down, fellows. Three white males, Walt." The lieutenant pushed reading glasses up on the bridge of his nose, leaned forward, picked up a file and answered Walter's query before it was delivered. "Jamie Mansfield, eighteen, Ronny McAlister, sixteen, and Lee Sumner, fifteen. All with priors, mainly petty shit. Guess they felt the need to graduate. Won't be long now. They're running out of time and common sense." He tossed the manilla folder back on the desk, sat back in his chair. "How's your family?"

"She's getting better. Sherry called from the hospital, said there was some response. But she still has a ways to go."

"That's great news, Walt. She'll make it," the lieutenant reaffirmed, then seemed to change thoughts in mid-sentence. "Any suspects in the Williamson murder?"

Detective Hardegree crossed his legs. "Well, right now, Pete, a Lucas Witherspoon, thirty-year-old Black male, lover, ex-lover, of the victim, right now we're not sure, supposed to be employed at Orinco Aluminum, is our prime suspect."

"Find 'im. Get him in 'the tomb.'" Lieutenant Peters

removed his glasses and laid them on the desk. "Is there anything else I need to know about this?"

Both detectives shook their heads.

"Well, detectives, there is something that you both need to know about." Peters plucked a lone sheet of paper off his desk, waited for Walter to grab it from his hand, but not before he had finished what he wanted to say. "We received this fax this morning and it's just a matter of time before it'll be all over the press. So, watch your backs. And at all times, keep your eyes and ears open."

Walter read the document from top to bottom and ran his hand through his hair before passing it to his partner, who grimaced after reading only the first five sentences.

"How do we know this is not a hoax, Pete?" Walter queried.

"The same way we don't know if it is, Walt." The weightiness of the lieutenant's words and his penetrating eye contact with his detective filled the silence with a tacit understanding. "But you don't get the big bucks for nothing. I'm sure you'll be the first to figure it out." Detectives Robinson and Hardegree rose and were headed out of the door. "Hey, Walt. You look terrible. Close the Williamson case so you can take your ass home, will ya?"

While Detective Hardegree ran criminal checks on Witherspoon, Walter hung his jacket on the back of his chair, sat at his desk, removed the beeper and Telissa Williamson's diary from the evidence bag, and placed them on the desk. He'd been round the block enough times to know that the killer would try to beep Telissa in order to cover his tracks, the same way a bank robber would call the police station to report his car being stolen moments after the robbery. Whoever it was who would beep Telissa now, nine out of ten they would be suspect number one. So he waited, concentrating on the beeper, almost willing it to sound, as if he were a medium trying to retrieve messages from the deceased.

After an hour, his thoughts had all converged upon one another without direction or purpose, creating chaos with his concentration. He found himself thinking more about his grandmother, his wife, the fax Pete had given him, than solving the case. He opened Telissa's diary to the page marked by the ink pen. She had addressed each day's entry, "Dear Telissa."

08/13
This has been a wonderful hot day. But God you are so good and I thank you for everything. I am blessed to have seen another day. I am healthy, my family is well and I have a job that I enjoy. This whole year has been a blessing. My mother, sister and I have never been closer. When I think about it, it all seems like a dream. I get a college degree and the job I want in the same month. Teaching kids is what I want to do with the rest of my life. I feel like there is nothing I can't accomplish and that no one can stop me from achieving my ultimate goal of starting my own school one day. I understand clearly that the past is the past and it is no use holding onto something that has no future. That's why, tomorrow, I'll end the relationship. Hopefully, he'll understand. If not—

"Hey, Walt!"

Walter would've known that voice if he were on a street corner in a big city during rush hour on a Friday afternoon on the planet Uranus. Jerry Riggs had just passed the sergeant's exam and was exhibiting symptoms of an acute case of ass-on-shoulders disease. He was on a fast track to lieutenant, past colonel, and maybe even chief of the force, possessing all of the qualities that the bosses prized—height, charm, good looks and the adeptness to cover up the worst of departmental fuck-ups.

"What was it in the Williamson case, drugs, prostitution or both?" He stood inches from Walter's desk, sipping coffee out of a Styrofoam cup.

"Neither," Walter barked, not looking up from his reading.

Sergeant Riggs held his drink waist level, away from his body. "You gotta be joking. Right?"

"I have no sense of humor."

"Listen, Robinson." Sergeant Riggs set his coffee on a nearby table. "A young Black gal found killed with nothing in her system? Are you sure? What did the pharmacology test show?"

Walter looked at Sergeant Riggs for the first time. "The test didn't show a goddam thing." He closed the diary. "Let me ask you something, Sergeant, why are you so sure drugs were involved?"

"What's else could it have been? Did she have any priors for prostitution?"

Walter shook his head and laughed. "You're a racist bastard. You know that?"

Sergeant Riggs took one step forward. "And I'm also

your immediate supervisor, Robinson. Watch your lip."

Walter stood up, moved inches from Riggs' face. "You think that all Black folks are junkies or whores? Just plain old criminals, huh, Sarge?"

"The ones we deal with anyway." He had a warped smile upon his face. "Just go down to the basement. Ninety-five percent of the people in lockup are your brothers and sisters, Robinson. It's your people that are committing the crimes. Hell, if ninety-five percent of your people are committing the crimes, why is everybody so bent out of shape about profiling? Profiling is good police work. Just think where this country would be without it."

"Wow." Walter rubbed his forehead with the tips of his fingers. "Ignorance is so underrated. You know what? I believed you were taught to be a racist, but you had to be born an asshole. It just comes too natural for you, Sarge—"

"Watch—"

"But I tell you what should be a crime, though. You wearing that goddam Sergeant's badge or any kind of badge for that matter. That's criminal."

The more the duo raised their voices the more attention they attracted in the squad room from co-workers, whose fingers froze on computer keyboards, stopped telephone conversations in mid-sentence or gaped with opened mouths.

Sergeant Riggs had his finger at eye level with Walter's face. "Listen, boy…I'm gonna write your ass up. You can't talk to me that way. Hardegree should be the lead on this case anyway. Don't take it out on me 'cause of your grandmama," he pronounced the word 'grandmama' as if it left a bad taste in his mouth, "caught a bad break. Who said life was fair? Anyway, after tonight, your ass'll be writing parking tickets. Uppity sonofabitch."

The expression on Walter's face was a mixture of anger at what was said to him and bewilderment that it was said at all. But the one word that sounded over and over was "boy," resonating like a ripple upon the surface of his mind. He grabbed Sergeant Riggs by his jacket lapels and jammed him hard into the wall, creating a commotion of raised voices, scrabbling feet, unintelligible expletives, earnest pleas and protruding arms separating the two. Walter broke the grip of two of his fellow officers, yanked his revolver from his holster and aimed it at Sergeant Riggs' head. Riggs was backed against the wall, surprised and fearful, as if he faced a firing squad without a blindfold.

"Shoot 'im, Walt!" Lieutenant Peters flung open his office door, striking the entire squad room with a paralysis of motion and sound. "Shoot him!"

The lieutenant pulled his own gun from his holster, stomped over to Sergeant Riggs and slapped it in his hand. "Go ahead, Riggs. Blow his goddam brains out." Sergeant Riggs looked at his hand as though he'd never seen a gun before, handed it back to the lieutenant. Robinson holstered his weapon, returned to his desk.

"Yeah," the lieutenant bellowed, "just what I thought. One of the first rules of being a cop," the crowd began to disperse, "is that you are to fight crime, not each other. Understand?" He turned, had words for Sergeant Riggs that were quiet with harshness and intensity. "Robinson! In my office. Now!"

Minutes later, Walter was kicked out of Lieutenant Peters' office like Jonah being spat from the belly of the whale. Detective Hardegree was waiting, standing, his legs crossed at the ankles, waving a sheet of paper as if it were a white flag. He stepped into Walter's path, obstructing his progress. "Walt. You won't believe this. Let's go over here." He guided him by the elbow in the direction of the break room. Caldwell and Cobb, both rookies, were huddled over a table comparing notes on the variation of experience.

"...like last night," Cobb was saying, "dispatcher gets a call from a woman, approximately mid-forties, who says she is the victim of a man who flashed her through her window. Me and Wilkerson arrive about twenty minutes later and interview the woman—"

"Don't tell me," Caldwell interrupted, "the guy was outside the window when you got there?"

"No. But check this out. We get there, right, and the woman takes us to her bathroom to show us where the incident occurred and Wilkerson and I look out of the window and in the adjacent house is a guy standing in front of his bathroom mirror shaving—the only part of him visible is his arms and chest in a t-shirt. Finally, Wilkerson and I look at each other and I say, 'Ma'am there's just a guy shaving in his own bathroom, he can't flash you from there, and even if he did you wouldn't be able to see anything from here.' She says, 'Oh yeah,' and slides a wooden crate from beneath her own bathroom sink and says, 'If you stand on this here box you can get a better look and you won't miss nothing he's got." Both officers pound their fists upon the table, Caldwell punching Cobb in the arm.

"Did y'all run her in?" Caldwell managed between guffaws.

"Uh-uh. Gave her a stepladder instead and some binoculars."

Detective Hardegree poured two cups of coffee while Walter thumbed through the headlines of the daily news. The lead story was the attack upon his grandmother and Walter had a sensation of floating high above the world, a detached observer sitting in a sidewalk café watching life stroll by. He was two paragraphs into the article when Detective Hardegree took the paper out of his hands and replaced it with a steaming cup of Java; he flipped the daily into the trash and sat opposite his partner, trying to cool his own beverage with intermittent blasts of breath. "The hell with that crap. Listen, Walt," he expounded, "three years ago Lucas Witherspoon was charged with assault."

Walter swallowed, licked his lips. "And?"

"With a knife." Detective Hardegree added cream, stirred.

"Telissa Williamson?"

"One and the same."

Walter set his cup upon the table and wiped his mouth with the back of his hand. "Let me ask you something, Detective. Why are we sitting here drinking badass coffee on one of hottest days of the year?"

Detective Hardegree hunched his shoulders, smiled. "Thought you could use a break."

"You're such a clever sonofabitch. Let's go catch a killer."

In one motion, Walter shoved Telissa's diary into his desk drawer and swooped his jacket off the back of his chair. He was halted in his tracks by Telissa's pager leaping off his desk. He inspected the number closely and decided to check it out from their unmarked squad car, before both men detoured to Central Supply to retrieve bullet-proof vests and additional ammo.

At 9.30 p.m., the night was thick, heavy, saturated with humidity, like a dusky sponge absorbing every ounce of initiative and energy until men lolled on street corners with anger bubbling beneath asphalt; or teenagers cruised in convertibles racing against boredom and bravado; or women slipped out of undergarments diving into pools creating concentric circles for a final lap. Detectives moved amongst and through it with all diligence and familiarity as though it were only a variation of yesterday and the day before that.

"What the hell is wrong with white folks, Joe?"

Walter turned from Allen Avenue onto North Fairground, checked his rearview mirror to make sure the two squad cars were following his lead.

"Are we going there again, Walt?" Detective Hardegree rattled the keyboard of a laptop computer.

"No." Walter lit a cigarette, cracked a window slightly. "We don't have to go anywhere. We've been there for the last four hundred years." He blew out the match, dumped it in the ashtray. "I don't know. Maybe Riggs was onto something. What d'you think?"

Detective Hardegree stopped typing, looked his partner squarely in the face. "I think Riggs is a jerk, Walt. He had no right to even mention your grandmother. If he's onto anything it's stupidity."

"But the sonofabitch is right, Joe. Most of the people we bust are Black."

"What color they are is not my first priority. They kill

'em, we catch 'em." He looked back at his monitor as if he were addressing it. "Like this sonofabitch right here. He's already caught."

"You telling me that when you cuff a guy and read him his rights you don't know what color he is?" Walter's voice was edged with incredulity.

Detective Hardegree shook his head. "I'm not saying that, Walt. I'm saying I just try to leave color out of the job. It's hard enough as it is."

Robinson rolled the window halfway down, flung the butt into the gutter. "So, the question that bothers me, which bothers me more now since Riggs brought it up, is if Blacks fill the jails more than any other group, are they predisposed to do so?" He let the question hang in the air like succulent fruit dangled before the face of the original man.

"Why do you insult me like that, Walt?" Detective Hardegree typed additional data into the laptop.

"What?"

Detective Hardegree's voice raised an octave in anger. "You act like there's no such thing as poverty, man. Or environmental conditions. Anyway, as far as I'm concerned, I only deal with good guys and bad guys." He smacked the computer for emphasis of point and impetus for quicker response.

"And I take it that I'm one of the good guys?"

"Right now, I'm not so sure."

Walter hung a left from North Fairground onto Holland.

"Now why do you insult me, Joe?"

"Damn!" Detective Hardegree read the information on the computer screen as if he were watching a tennis match.

"That phone number on Telissa's beeper was a payphone." He snapped the laptop shut with a pop, giving undivided attention to his partner. "Insult you?"

Walter's voice rose in intensity. "Hell, yeah. What's wrong with recognizing me as a Black man? Before I became a detective, I was Black." He was pointing to imaginary persons in imaginary places. "I mean, what's wrong with recognizing that guy as being Chinese or her for being Hispanic or him for being whoever the hell he is. When you don't, you're saying that person doesn't exist, or at best is on the fringe of existence. One big melting pot? Well, hell, if you melt everything down in one big pot, its got to come out white. At least in America. I prefer," he pontificated with his head cocked at an angle, "to look at this thing as one big salad. You got all these different ethnic groups or ingredients, right, that go into making this one dish. Each ingredient maintains its own peculiar characteristics while going into the total makeup of the dish. Either way you have to recognize all the ingredients for what they are and the more you have the more rich and wonderful the salad will be." He came to a four-way stop, waited for another vehicle to proceed, then continued. "But hey, the way it is and the way it should be ain't got a damn thing to do with each other."

Detective Hardegree looked out of his window and said, as if talking to no one in particular, "You still want to be partners, Walt?"

"Why the hell wouldn't I want to be?"

"I don't know. Sounds like you got a beef with white people and I'm one of 'em so that means you got a beef with me."

Walter chuckled to himself. "Yeah. You're white alright. I saw you trying to dance at the Christmas party. You're about as white as they get, buddy. But I ain't got no beef with you for that. I recognize and respect your whiteness and therefore I have to respect you as a human being. My problem is with a system that puts more value on the color of your whiteness than it does on life itself. Matter of fact, so much value has been given to it that whiteness is a God masquerading as Christianity."

"Let's leave the religion thing alone, Walt." Detective Hardegree double-checked his weapon, re-holstered it. "And while you're at it, leave the goddam country alone too, willya? I mean, where else in the hell would you wanna live? Iraq, Zimbabwe, China? This country, it has its faults. It has its up and downs. But it's a great country. We're so goddam spoiled we don't realize how good we have it."

Walter veered into the left lane and waited for a stream of cars to zoom by before turning left onto Grand Avenue. "Well, what about all that bullshit about 'life, liberty and the pursuit of happiness' and something about 'all men being created equal. That's the kind of stuff that makes a country great, not how much wealth or bombs it accumulates. See, you can't write a bunch of bullshit like that and have it not include everybody. But that's what has happened and continues to happen and that's the reason why we're in the fix we're in." He swallowed and uttered a final sentence. "You've seen it yourself, war or no war, good economy or natural disasters, this race thing is only gettin' worse."

Walter eased the white Cavalier to a stop at 26 North Grand Avenue. The two patrol cars followed his cue and all three vehicles flipped off their headlights. Walter unfastened his seatbelt and had his door halfway open with one foot on the ground, the interior of the car bursting into light.

"Wait a minute, Walt, goddammit." Detective Hardegree had his partner's forearm in his grip. "When the hell have you never been included in anything? You're college educated, a detective with a good salary, a nice home in the suburbs, a pretty wife. Man, you've got all the trappings of success. What the hell you got to bitch about? Do you think you would have accomplished all that if it hadn't been for this country? I don't know," he threw his hands in the air as if he were through with the whole affair, "maybe you want to be the savior of the Black race. Is that it, Walt? And another thing, the constitution and Declaration of Independence of this country are great words written by great men. And, oh yeah, inspired by God. That's not bullshit."

Walter slammed the car door, plunging the two into darkness. "Let me tell you something about success, Joe. I've succeeded, if you wanna call it that, in spite of America. I've always worked twice as hard, made sure I spoke proper English when I had to, wore the best suits, rubbed elbows with the snobbiest of bastards, and all of that has only gotten me so far. Hell, I trained that sonofabitch Riggs, remember? And now he's my super. And when I'm off duty, my fellow officers pull me over with some bullshit about broken taillights or illegal lane changes just to search my vehicle. You know how many times I've had guns pulled on me by my fellow officers while I'm off duty and the next day those sonofabitches are laughing behind my back? More than I can count. If that's your idea of success, I'm on the top of the mountain, man. I say half an American dream is like being kissed and punched at the same time. Every day you have to decide whether to pucker up or duck. And as far as being a Black savior goes..."

Four uniformed officers were standing outside Walter's window in SWAT gear, impatience in their eyes, agitation about their movements. Walter held up one finger, turned his attention back to his partner, "...that will never work. My hair is too kinky, lips too full and skin too black. Black folks'll never go for a savior that looks like that." He checked his own weapon. "Show time, partner."

Detective Hardegree and a uniformed officer covered the rear escape, two other officers manned opposite ends of the street and Walter and a pimply-faced rookie, O'Connor, approached the front steps of the apartment. A small crowd formed under streetlights and by stop signs; neighbors craned their necks out of windows and around corners.

"He ain't here."

A middle-aged Black woman in a blue cotton dress sat on an opposite porch, a bottle of beer beside her chair and Howling Wolf wafting from inside her own apartment. She was combing and twisting handfuls of hair into a masterpiece of braids on the head of a teenage girl sitting between her knees, who shifted uneasily between grimace and silence. She wore gray shorts and a blue strapless top.

"Who ain't here?" Walter inquired from ten feet away, shining the beam of the flashlight into the woman's face.

Without looking up, she dipped her index finger into a can of hair grease and slid it along the teenager's scalp. "Whoever you're looking for. And could you please get that light outa my face."

"Where is he?" Walter had one foot on the first step, his flashlight now turned off, his left hand resting on his thigh.

"Who?"

"Who it is we're looking for."

"Ah, him." She made eye contact with the officers, reached down to strangle the beer bottle and took a long swig. "Left early this morning with work clothes on. Look like he was going to work."

O'Connor wiped the back of his neck with a handkerchief; Walter spat in the gutter.

"I reckon so. How did you know it was him that we were looking for?"

"You sure as hell wasn't looking for me." She took another long swallow and set the bottle down with a thud on the wooden porch. "Anyway, he didn't do it."

"Didn't do what, ma'am?"

With a black plastic comb she plowed more furrows of fallow scalp in anticipation of a harvest of braids. "What he's accused of."

"Then what did he do?"

"That I couldn't say. I guess we're all guilty of something." She glanced up at him with an accusatory squint.

"OK." Walter gave instructions into the walkie-talkie in his right hand and a static-filled, garbled, affirmative reply came back. He tapped on the door with his flashlight, announced his presence. And again, and a third time, without any answer.

"Told ya he wasn't there."

Walter radioed his team and skipped down the steps

without looking back. "Tell your son we'll be back, ma'am."

"Hey," she called, pausing with her hand in mid-air, wielding the comb like a cutlass. "You like pig's feet?"

Walter about-faced, slowly. "No, ma'am. I'll pass on them feet. Ain't no tellin' where that pig been stepping."

"Ah, hell. Don't worry about that. You're a detective. You suppose to have all the answers."

"Yeah." He nodded, smiled, turned towards the direction of the unmarked car. "Have a good night, ma'am."

"I gots greens and sweet potatoes too!"

Gradually the crowd scattered like wisps of cigarette smoke as the officers gathered and engaged in a impromptu debriefing bull session. There were guffaws, curses, spitting and talk about paperwork back at the station, cold ones and impending vacation days filled with the sound of trout splashing in cold stream waters. And occasionally someone mentioned the name of the suspect and checking with his employer and how they probably wouldn't find him there either because as soon as they left his mother would be on the phone to him warning about the police.

Walter sat on the curb, trying to rub fatigue from his eyes; he yawned, battling exhaustion more than sleep. Detective Hardegree squatted beside him.

"Why don't you call it a night, Walt? The scent is still fresh. We'll pick up the trail tomorrow."

Walter raised his head, fixed his mouth in a determined set. "We need to check out his mother's apartment."

Detective Hardegree looked in the direction of the duplexes. "Nah. He's not in there, Walt. Besides, we'll have to get another search warrant and I sure as hell don't wanna do that tonight."

Walter shook his head. "I'm not talking about no suspect, Joe. She's harboring greens and sweet potatoes, man." Then, as an afterthought, turning up his nose, "You like pig's feet?"

"Look," Detective Hardegree grabbed his partner under his right armpit, pulled him to his feet. "I don't know what you're talking about and I don't think you do either. Let's call it a night. I'll catch a ride back with McAdams and Pirtle. You able to drive?"

"I drove down here, didn't I?"

"Alright, buddy." He slapped Walter on the shoulder. "I'll see you tomorrow."

"Tomorrow, yes." Walter watched them retreat into their vehicles, execute U-turns and drive off, until their taillights became red blurs smearing the night with distance and dissolution.

Walter Robinson snapped off his tie and threw it and his jacket into the back seat. He closed his eyes and leaned his head upon the headrest. It felt good just to be still and do nothing but breathe. Thoughts of his grandmother came to his mind like a haunting melody of a pop song played in heavy rotation. He probably should swing by the hospital to check on Big Mama, but that would only induce pangs of depression. She had always represented strength, courage, and grace in his life, and now those attributes had senselessly been stripped away, revealing a vulnerability and a weakness that were foreign and emotionally debilitating. And every time he felt that way waves of anger gathered around his ankles, swelled in his stomach and rushed towards his brain, threatening to blow the top of his skull off. At times like this he had an almost uncontrollable urge to hurt someone or something or maybe even himself, or find a vacant field and try to out scream the rage ripping him apart. During all of his time on the force, he'd always prided himself on being a model of consistency, strength, and stability, the consummate cop. But the past forty-eight hours had grabbed a handful of his manhood and held it up to the light for analysis and scrutiny. Was he who he had projected himself to be? Did he really believe in the principles he espoused? Had he lost himself chasing suspects down some dark alley? And did any of it really matter any more? He had to get his emotional house in order. The whole world has problems. In police work there are no gray areas. You either get the job done or you don't.

Walter straightened his back in the seat and cranked the ignition. He flipped off the air conditioner, rolled down the windows and screeched his tires upon acceleration. The city, like all cities, had its own rhythm, pulse, and attitude. It was a living, breathing organism. He could have stuck his hand out of the window and physically touched it. The traffic, the noise, the lights. He turned right onto Winchester, headed for Bryant Towers Public Housing. These streets and the people that inhabited them were as familiar to him as his favorite chair in front of the evening news after supper. He knew the tacit mores, body language, facial expressions, how death could result from scuffing someone's shoes or over leather jackets or wrong colors or staring at someone too hard, too long. And he knew where to find his nephew, Eric Merriweather, aka Cebo, leader of the Gangster Apostles, who was of these streets. Right after Walter's sister, Cassandra, left unannounced in the middle of the night, he tried to reach his nephew, but the lure of these streets, like a voluptuous woman doing a striptease, was too much for a fourteen-year-old boy with their promises of easy money, violence, and guns, and he'd often wondered what would have become of him upon these streets had Big Mama not been there. Actually, Cassandra was adopted by Big Mama when she was teenaged and pregnant with nowhere to go, and that made her Walter's adopted sister and Cebo his adopted nephew. But as far as he was concerned they were of the same blood, no matter how many labels you put on it. Cebo had known jail cells, emergency rooms, near-death experiences. He was eighteen now, hardened and battle-tested by these streets, and this was the life he'd chosen, and while Walter didn't condone his actions, he respected his nephew because he had juice in the community, misguided though it was; nothing went down in Bryant Towers without Cebo's knowledge.

Walter turned into the entrance of the public housing project. If you have seen one, he reflected, you've seen them all. Right, some differ in height and width but they all were built upon the same foundation of poverty, hopelessness, and helplessness. Modern-day reservations for self-hate and self-destructive behavior. It seemed ironic to Walter that no matter in what American city he ventured the majority of Black folk were confined to certain sections to become neighbors with high unemployment, poor schools, and even worse housing. Or maybe it wasn't so ironic at all.

He noticed some kids playing catch and heard them give warning whistles at the same time. Yep, the whole projects knew he was in the house now. It was their way of blowing trumpets and rolling out red carpets. He circled the complex, came to a stop near the playground, clipped a cell phone onto his belt, and got out of the car. From a nearby parked '64 Impala, stereo speakers thumped a hip hop beat, rattling windows. Two girls in shorts and sandals sat in lawn chairs on a porch, the aroma of marijuana drifting through the air like the sweetness of a lotus blossom. Around the corner of one building, four youths were passing bottles of wine, shooting craps, and cursing them. Usually when he approached someone shouted "One time" and everyone would freeze like deer caught in headlights, ready to break or hide the evidence before Walter was upon them. But this time they stood to acknowledge his presence, tossed their heads at him, spitting "What's up?" out of the corners of their mouths, and one young man, bare chested, ebony skin glistening from perspiration and streetlights, proffered a half-empty bottle of wine.

"Nah, man." Walter squinted, trying to focus perception and motive. "What the hell is wrong with y'all? Where's 'Bo?"

Their eyes pointed in the direction of the playground. Walter moved away quickly, checking over his shoulder; he could've sworn those fellows were smiling at him.

"What's up, my niggahs?" Walter saluted a group of five youths lounging on swings and monkey bars with their leader holding court in the center of them.

"Hey, Uncle Walter," Cebo replied, his clique relaxing as if they'd been given an 'at ease' directive.

"Uncle Walter? So it's like that now? Don't nobody respect the police no more, huh? Alright, check this. Get your ass up against them monkey bars, Cebo. Go on, now!" He patted Cebo down roughly, spreading his legs farther and searching down to his ankles. "Ah hell, yeah." He pulled a .25-caliber handgun and a wad of cash out of Cebo's sock, spun the gun around his index finger before pocketing the money and the weapon. "Cute. Now the rest of y'all get the fuck out of here."

The Apostles held their positions, as though the earth they stood upon was hallowed ground.

Cebo looked over his shoulder, made a clicking sound through his teeth, dispersing his inner circle.

"Turn around," Walter ordered. "We need to talk, 'Bo."

Cebo brushed himself off. "How's Big Mama?"

"Why in hell did you send that fax down to the station?"

"What fax?"

They stood close enough to one another that Cebo could have counted the hairs in his uncle's nose. "Don't make me bust your ass like I should've done about ten years ago."

Cebo expanded his chest in warning. "You answer my question, I'll answer yours."

"She's hanging in there."

"Bet." He started walking away from Walter, trailing his words behind him. "Let's go over here and sit down, man."

Cebo wore a black flannel shirt and khaki pants that barely hugged his hips, sagging upon unlaced sneakers, and Walter Robinson knew that by his shirttail being out it concealed underwear that otherwise would have been gaudily displayed. He was of medium height, slight build, light complexioned with a large, well-groomed Afro and a mole on his left cheek. They found seats on the swing set where the grass had been eaten away by adolescent feet shoving off into the stratosphere and skidding to a stop upon re-entry and dismount.

"We got your fax, 'Bo."

"What fax?" He spat into the dust.

"The one you sent to the police station saying in forty-eight hours a cop would be shot and another every day until the attackers of Dissie Marshall were arrested and prosecuted."

"What makes you think it was me?"

"'Cause you can't spell worth a shit. Even when you were a kid and I was tutoring your ass you couldn't spell then and you still can't. You left out an R in arrested."

"I ain't admitting nothing and I ain't denying nothing." He shook his head morosely from side to side. "It's hard to understand why some words are that way, though. Seems like a waste of letters to me."

"Maybe I was a poor teacher. Anyway, you're the only one bold enough to try and pull some shit like that."

Cebo shook his head, turned his lips into a pout. "Big Mama was my grandmother too, Uncle Walter. It doesn't matter if words were misspelled or if it was King James's English. You got the point and the white boys downtown did too. They sent you down here, didn't they?" He cut a sidewards glance that landed upon Walter like a shadow.

"Watch your mouth, 'Bo. And let me ask you something while I'm at it: what line of work you think I'm in? You talking about shooting cops, you better pray you don't miss this cop. 'Cause I'll put a fax out of my own and I'll deliver it personally right between your eyes. You want a war, 'Bo? That what you want?"

Cebo held up both hands, trying to dam the flow of Walter's words. "Not with you, Uncle Walter. You're blood. Matter of fact, me and you can do some thangs together, shake up some shit around here. I've been studying and thinking and organizing and drawing up plans." His words became heavier from the seriousness in his voice. "See, that's what's wrong with niggers. We got all these so-called leaders that can give a good speech, but don't nobody never plan nothing worth a damn. And when you're unorganized, you're always at the mercy of somebody else." He added as an afterthought, "But it can happen."

"What can happen?"

"The end of suffering for Black people."

Walter was becoming exasperated, expelled a long sigh to prove it. "The end of what? Man, you gotta be kiddin'. But amuse me some more and tell me you just planning to kill white cops or will a Black one do just the same? And how is killing anybody gonna make anything right?"

"I said it once and I'll say it again: I ain't admitting nothing and I ain't denying nothing." He flashed a sardonic smile before becoming serious. "But I will tell you this: out here on these streets right ain't got nothing to do with it. You know that, Uncle Walter. It's all juice and props. We give and take our own justice, man. You think those white boys gonna do any time for what they did to Big Mama? All the white boys I know that get busted with dope go to rehab, not jail. I doubt if the cops are even looking for 'em. Not seriously anyway. If a white girl say she been raped by a Black dude, they pick up every nigger from here to New York and harass his ass. Now, you let a sister get raped and she had to be asking for it, right? And as far as white cops versus Black cops go, when they come around here, it ain't no difference. Matter of fact, the Black cops, a lot of 'em anyway, are more brutal 'cause that's the way they impress the white boys and get a few scraps thrown at them back downtown; I ain't tellin' you nothin' new, Uncle Walter. We know who come around here to intimidate and terrorize. If somebody made all the bastards disappear, I wouldn't lose no sleep over it. But hey," Cebo held up both hands in surrender, "I ain't admitting nothin' and I ain't denying nothin'. But I do know, ain't nobody gonna fuck with you. So, you talk about one thing don't make another thing right—around this way, you make your own right or you don't make it at all."

Walter shook his head. "Look at me, man." He grabbed his nephew's chin in his hand and turned his face towards him. "Does it look like I'm out hunting the bushes, playing Charles Bronson? If anybody should be it should be me, and if I ain't taking revenge your little ass shouldn't either. Even white folks is upset about this thing. Them white boys ain't got nowhere to hide. And let me ask you this: where you and your crew gonna hide when the Forrest Police Department start kicking down doors and cracking heads? You don't know what brutal is 'Bo. But you about to find out. It's just a matter of time before they trace that fax, and don't you know that they gonna ride on you or whoever the hell sent it before any deal goes down?"

"I would be surprised if they didn't." Cebo turned from

his uncle's hand, pulled a comb from his back pocket, ran it through his hair. "That's the nature of the beast. If it wasn't for me and the homeboys, the beast wouldn't have nobody to keep down."

"That's bullshit. You and your homeboys keep your own selves down. You can't blame white man for everything, 'Bo."

Cebo laughed aloud. "You're right. If we start spreading the blame it should be shared between the white man and so-called middle-class Negroes trying their best to be white." He stuck the comb in his back pocket.

"Hey." Walter slowly got to his feet, his voice rising like an omen. "You got something to say to me stand on your feet and take your ass-whipping like a man."

Cebo was half laughing, smiling. "Uncle Walter, Uncle Walter, relax baby." He was trying to pull his uncle back into the swing seat. "I ain't got no beef with you, baby. We're kinfolks. Chill on that."

"Damn straight." Robinson grabbed his nephew in a headlock before sitting back down. "I'll take that tree limb over there and beat you like you stole something, boy." He tightened the vice around Cebo's head and then released him.

"Alright, man. I hear ya." Cebo patted his Afro back into place. "You know I ain't got nothing but love for you, man. When Mama split, you was the only family that reached out to me. I know you didn't have to do that. My coward-ass daddy wasn't man enough to do it and everybody else was scared to. You gave me a place to stay, took me here and there, tried to hip me to the right way of doing things, and you might've thought I wasn't paying attention but I still remember the symphony, the museums and *Othello* you took me to. That was dope. If I'd known then what I know now, I wouldn't have gotten caught up in this thang. But hey, I don't cry over nothing I can't change. It all worked out, Uncle Walter. I found a family, a real family once and for all, and they give me all the love and respect I need." He watched two kids shooting a basketball towards a goal with chain links for nets. "How's Aunt Sherry?"

"She's fine."

"Cool." Cebo redirected the waters of the conversation back to their original course. "Shee-it. You the man, Uncle Walter. You played the game and came out on top man. You got position, status, juice. I see your ass on TV all the time busting somebody. Homeboys all over the city know and respect you. But not because you this or that or 'cause you living in the hills or got a nice bank. You wanna know why?" He didn't give his uncle time to part his lips. "'Cause you ain't afraid of your own people, man. You a homeboy. Look at you. You ain't scared to come down here or go anywhere else for that matter. And when you do come around the way you ain't wearing no social worker hat or looking down on nobody or coming down here delivering sermons or trying to pimp nobody or no bullshit like that. If you say something then that shit might as well be set in concrete, 'cause that's what you mean. Hell, we can relate to that shit. You treat us like human beings, know what I'm saying? I can look in your eyes and tell you know where I'm coming from. We might be on two different sides of the field, but we're playing the same game. We're the same folks, man. Fuck that uncle-and-nephew shit. More like brothers, especially since what went down with Big Mama."

Walter lit a cigarette, took a long slow drag and released the smoke skyward. He blew out the match, tossed it into the dirt. "Are you through?"

Cebo stared ahead, watching as one kid shaked and baked the other kid, dribbled between his legs before going in and laying the ball off the backboard and through the hoop. Nice.

"Listen," Walter continued, "first of all, where in hell do you think I'm from? I was raised in neighborhoods like this until I went and lived with Big Mama. Hell, I almost joined a gang myself. Why should I be afraid?"

"Hey." Cebo jumped in. "I know a lot of people that was raised around here that done made it. But money, cars, and clothes sometimes got a way of making you forget your raising. We don't let some people come around here now unless they got a ghetto pass. Being afraid or not being afraid is a matter of choice. But hey, I ain't mad at nobody. You gotta do whatcha gotta do. Know what I'm sayin'?"

"No, I don't know whatcha sayin', 'Bo. You talking 'bout we like brothers and we're the same…that bullshit is so deep I should be wearing boots." He offered Cebo a cigarette.

"I roll my own."

"I don't know any brothers that sell dope to their own people or shoot and kill their own people 'cause you live on one side of town and I live on the other and we fighting over colors and street corners that neither one of us will ever own. Fear is not the only thing that is a matter of choice. Nah, Cebo. We a long way from being alike. We better stick to the uncle-and-nephew relationship. It's a lot safer for both of us that way."

"That's what I'm sayin', Uncle Walter. That was yesterday. Thangs is changin'. It's peace in the Middle East."

"What does that mean?"

Cebo's voice increased in pitch from excitement. He beamed like a kid at Christmas time. "Big Mama. Since the thang with Big Mama, the brothers done called a truce. We ain't fightin' each other no more. We've being knowing the enemy for years. But now we know what he looks like. I tell you, Uncle Walter," he exercised his legs on the swing as if warming up for takeoff, "this thing feels right, like being able to see for the first time. In the past we was just fighting and killing to be fighting and killing. But we ain't in the dark no more. We see the real enemy now. And he looks a helluva lot better between the cross-hairs of a semi-automatic, where he should've been a long time ago."

"Goddam." Walter threw down his cigarette. "You and the homeboys just signed your death warrant, 'Bo. What in hell y'all thinking about? You got semi-automatics and the white man got M-16s and tanks." He stomped upon his cigarette butt glowing in the dust.

"Ain't no thang, Uncle Walter. I've seen the face of Death. It ain't no uglier than life on these streets." He stood to his feet. "Well, I wasn't the brightest math student in class but tomorrow night will be forty-eight hours and like that fax said, they either catch the cowards or it's on. I just hope nobody gets impatient before the forty-eight hours are up." His words carried the blunt force of a threat.

"Meaning?"

"Meaning that a lot of people around here got a habit of saying fuck the police. Might be some fax-sender sympathizers, man. You never know. Haha. But in the meantime, man, if your buddies come looking for us and take us out, that's cool. Why should we be any more important than Huey, George Jackson, or Malcolm. You taught me about them, remember?"

"You don't know nothing." Walter stood to his feet, squaring off with his nephew as if they were two pugilists in the center of the ring. "Look, 'Bo. For the last time, I don't need no help. Back the fuck off. This ain't the 1960s, that struggle is over with. People have already bled and died for the opportunities you refuse to take advantage of. You little motherfuckers don't know nothing 'bout fighting for freedom. It's a different time, it's a different set of circumstances, and it's a different world. Just back the fuck off."

"I can't argue with that. It probably is a different world. But don't nothing never change. Look, man, no white person is gonna call me nigger to my face any more. They don't have to. The judges and lawyers and banks and schools and doctors and real estate folks will do it for 'em without sayin' a word. Far as I can tell, Uncle Walter, as long as you're Black the struggle won't ever be over. I'm sorry you're in the middle of this thang, man, but you don't have to be."

"What's that supposed to mean?"

"Meaning like I said before. You're a homeboy. We're gonna need more weapons, surveillance equipment, shit like that. I know you hate them white bastards just as bad as we do now. Think about it."

"'Bo. You done lost your goddam mind out here, man. You need to think about this. You know it's just a matter of time before one of your homeboys rolls over on your little ass and I nail you for a murder rap out here on these streets. Or better yet, when the heat comes down, and believe me it's on the way, I'll be one of the ones kicking your door in hunting you down. You know that, don'tcha?"

"Would that be right?"

"Like you said. Right ain't got nothing to do with it."

"Yeah, I did say that, didn't I? Never could get shit past my Uncle Walter. But check this: whether I kill cops or they shoot me down in the streets, look around." Cebo's arm traced a panoramic arc over the neighborhood. "What do I have to lose?"

Walter reached into his pocket, pulled out the .25 automatic, removed the clip, and handed the hollow weapon to Cebo. He turned and threw the clip into some weeds, walked away, and called over his shoulder. "Just back off, 'Bo."

"You give a man a gun without any bullets? That's wrong, man. That's just plain wrong, but it's alright. It's a brand-new day. We'll make our own ammo."

Walter shook his head, held up his hand without breaking stride.

"Uncle Walter! If I hear anything about who sent that fax, I'll holla."

Walter Robinson sat in his car for almost half an hour, smoking, counting the wad of cash he had taken off his nephew. Eight hundred dollar bills, two twenties, one ten. He reached into his back pocket, pulled out a well-worn wallet, stuffed the loot inside. The little bastard probably made that within the last hour, Walter thought to himself. It wasn't hard out here in these streets to make some fast cash. At one point he was jacking dealers on a regular basis coming away with five, six grand a pop. It was either that or haul their little asses off to jail, which wasn't worth the time or effort, the dealers being back on the streets before he got through with the paperwork. So it was best to make them pay on the spot, a Walter Robinson tax. And if they refused, he would negotiate with them: the butt of his revolver against the side of their heads until they reached a mutual agreement. Who in the hell was a drug dealer going tell that he got robbed? The police? He thought of Cebo and laughed out loud. "I ain't admitting nothin' and I ain't denying nothin'." Trying to talk some sense into Cebo was an exercise in futility, his nephew just about as determined as they'd come. And why should he expect anything different? As much as he didn't want to admit it, they were too much alike. Once either of them believed in an idea, they attached their minds to it as if it were superglue. Must run in the family. Walter thought about all of the other kids with brilliant minds, not unlike his nephew, living in ghettoes, who could be entrepreneurs, CEOs or engineers. A wasteland of unfulfilled potential and cancelled dreams that put bargain-basement prices on the cycle of life. He'd talked to kids who considered themselves blessed just to live twenty-two years. Teenagers who exhibited symptoms of stress and trauma characteristic of war zones halfway around the world. Kids who had already prepared their funerals down to the finest of details, including the color of roses, songs, and burial suits. It's so easy to ride through and work around communities like this; one develops a detachment from the everyday pain and the people. Makes it more convenient to live your own life. His visits always ended with him like some B-movie cowboy riding off into a middle-class sunset, leaving behind a widening gap between Black folk and Black folk. Urbanization and technology had planted seeds of Black subculture within Black culture. The fruit being those that are dreamless and those that are one missed paycheck from dreamlessness, leaving a community divided, confused, and spiritually destitute. The people Walter knew around here were not all gang members or drug dealers. There were decent men going to work every day, trying to do the right thing and support families; the elderly, like Mrs Betty Deberry, whose last breath would probably be taken behind security doors and barred windows; young sisters fighting to stay off welfare rolls, working two or more jobs with very few benefits, if any, stretching take-home pay beyond possibility. And then there were kids who excelled academically, volunteered time and energy to help others, kids you didn't read about in the papers unless they were shooting dope, hoops, or bullets. In order to maintain sanity, Walter thought, you had to disengage yourself from the madness around you or risk going mad yourself. Even thinking about things too long could lead down a long winding road to depression. But hell, I didn't create this mess, I inherited it, he mused. And I damn sure can't save the world. Couldn't even save my own nephew. I need a drink, he thought to himself.

He drove two blocks eastward and pulled into the driveway of a small brick house with a light on in an upstairs window and a fern hanging from its porch. He rang the doorbell, listened to footfalls flipping and flopping in flat house shoes, the turn of keys in locks, the sound of metal and wood swinging on hinges, and then a slim dark-skinned woman in a silk bathrobe framed the doorway.

"Hey baby," she draped her arms around Walter Robinson's neck. "You look beat." She stood back to get a better look at him, hugged him again. "I didn't think you were coming."

"I tell you what," he felt her nipples harden against his chest, "you keep hugging me like this, I'm gonna come right now." With a kick of his right foot, he slammed the door shut. "I'm thirsty."

She pecked him on the lips. "Scotch on the rocks?"

He slapped her on her buttocks. "That'll work."

Walter Robinson removed the cell phone from his belt loop, sat on the couch and removed his shirt, using it for a towel. He called his wife, covering the mouthpiece with his hand. "Virginia. Just let me get a beer."

A voice answered throaty with drowsiness.

He spoke into the receiver. "Sherry?"

"Walter? I've been trying to call you. Are you alright? Where have you been?"

"Yeah. I'm fine. What's the latest with Big Mama?"

"That's what I've been trying to call you about. She's still in intensive, but she's talking a little now. She's asking for you. I left word for you at the station."

Emotion swelled within Walter Robinson's chest and lodged in his throat, obstructing words of joy and relief. He wiped his eyes and tried to swallow several times, seeking courage and air.

"Walter?"

"That's good news. Damn, that's good news. Listen…"

Virginia had returned from the kitchen bearing beer. She stood before Walter with the drink in her left hand, the bottle dripping beads of perspiration, patiently awaiting his undivided attention. He hit the mute button, secured the phone between his shoulder and ear and with both hands free untied her robe, watched it fall to the floor in undulating waves of grace. He fondled and kissed her breasts, nipples bright as a full moon on a winter's night. The sound of Sherry's voice droned in his ear like background music without melody or rhythm, a distraction against the silence, as Walter slid off Virginia's panties, silk and black also, admired the radiance of pubic hair, sweet smells of womanhood. She stood before him wearing only a belly ring and took a long swallow from his beer.

He hit the mute button again, reared back on the couch, and spoke into the mouthpiece "Uh, listen. I'm working late, baby. I caught a case. I need to stay on top of some things right now."

Virginia set the beer on the coffee table, fell to her knees, began to unbuckle Walter's pants, slide them and his underwear around his ankles.

"Are you going to check on Big Mama? Or does that damn job take precedence over everything?…What was that, Walter?"

"What was what? Look, don't start that shit right now, hear? I'll get by the hospital as soon as I can. If anything changes, call me."

"No. I'm through calling you. Goodbye." There was silence and then the hum of a dial tone.

"Sherry? Sherry? Damn."

Before Walter could hang up the phone, Virginia had

mysteriously produced a condom from mid-air. She tore its wrapper and began rolling it upon Walter's manhood, already stiff and throbbing. She mounted him and wrapped her arms around his neck, her passion increasing in intensity and velocity with each pelvic thrust, her tongue occasionally finding the sides of his neck and the wetness of his own mouth. It felt good. To have someone wrap their arms around you—without condoning or condemnation, holding on as if their life depended upon it, when in reality it's your life hanging in the balance and that embrace is enough to save you and make you hold on with equal fervor, at least for one fleeting moment—is to be alive. Virginia emitted a throaty moan and arched her back as Walter's head fall backwards against the couch, the cell phone slipping from his hand onto the floor, his beer flat and abandoned upon the table.

They moved into the bedroom. He loved the arch of her back, the roundness of her buttocks, and the sparkle in her eyes when she looked back at him when she was on all fours and he entered her. He controlled the tempo of lovemaking with both hands on her narrow waist, determined when he wanted to drive or have her take the wheel, left a print on her ass from the slap of his hand before closing his eyes and holding on tightly as if he were on a rollercoaster of ecstasy and exhilaration, about to break the bonds of gravity and be sucked into a cosmos of shooting stars, a universe of exploding planets beyond secrets of galaxies unknown.

Lying in the embers of spent passion, musk and wet spots, Virginia under his arm, Walter Robinson felt as though he could finally sleep.

"Hey. What happen to my beer?"

"I could use one myself." She smiled, kissed his chest. "I'll be right back."

With Virginia laying next to him, Walter Robinson sipped his beer, stared at the ceiling and thought: Damn, that was a good. But it was becoming the same old good the same old way each and every same old time and it was beginning to bore him. And the more he thought on it, he keep coming to the same conclusion: sex is so overrated, and silly too. The act almost never outweighs the thought of it. One, it's different each time you do it, not necessarily good. Two, you expend all of that energy and effort and five minutes later—if that long—it's over. Three, afterwards you wash up and leave or you lay around emotionally vulnerable, seeing your partner for the first time and vice versa, exposed to feelings of guilt or regret. The orgasm, Walter thought, should be in the imagination after the winking of an eye, the quick arch of eyebrows, the slow licking of lips, the ethereal touch on the hand, slow crossing of legs in miniskirts, the soft jingle of cleavage in low-cut blouses, space between shirttail and trousers revealing the flesh of the lower back and coquettish smiles on painted mouths. Too often the experience of lovemaking was reduced to grunt, ejaculation and deep sleep. One should never engage in sex without a sense of innocence lost.

Like those days of his seventeenth summer on Big Mama's farm. Charlene Spearman stayed the next road over, was a freshman entering the University of Tennessee, and loved picnics in the cool of the day. They'd met crossing trails on the backs of horses, and somehow his horse always managed to get out of the stable, wandering to her house, where he'd have to retrieve it. There had been movies, baseball games, and church, but this day she'd packed cold chicken and potato salad, planning an afternoon down by the pond. He remembered the afternoon smelled yellow. The flowers, sunshine, breeze lapping off the water. They talked of future plans, fed one another, held hands and walked. Inside the barn, their mouths merged, their tongues forging words of passion and desire. He'd felt girls up before, squeezed titties, pinched asses since junior high, even plunged his middle finger into moist pussy and wiped it under his nose. But this was something heavier than kids' stuff, like he was on the cusp of something he wanted but couldn't quite define. He suggested the loft and relished the sweat of Charlene's caramel skin, her mouth insatiable for his own, until their naked bodies glistened from the yellow summer heat and he spread her legs, revealing a treasure of diamonds sparkling and breathtaking. After two unsuccessful attempts, he plunged his hardness into her and began to run a hundred-meter sprint. "Slow, slow," she admonished, and they both began to share common rhythms and improvised movements to a brand-new dance upon a bed of yellow hay. Walter felt the world fall away beneath him as he floated towards the ceiling, his eyes closing involuntarily, his anus tightening, his toes stiffening and his mouth spewing guttural sounds. He jumped up in one motion, squeezing his penis as if he were trying to suture a wound, and scrambled down the loft ladder three rungs at a time. "What is wrong with you?" Charlene asked, peering over the edge of the hay loft. "I thought I had to pee," he replied, embarrassed, not looking up, spilling his semen on the ground. "Get back up here," she laughed and he complied, still holding his penis in his hand.

Virginia stirred, turned on her side, rolling Walter out of his reminiscence. He laughed quietly, took another swallow of the lukewarm beer, and massaged her shoulder. Her skin was thick with ebony, rich with a texture like gold. He loved the way it felt under his touch, and as they lay here under the faint light of the moon, a glow hovered over her like a guardian angel. He'd met Virginia the way he'd met most people in the 'hood: through death. Her only son, fifteen, was found in the back of a trunk, two gunshots execution style. He'd investigated, closed the case, and did his civic duty of consoling the bereaved mother. And they'd been comforting one another for the past eight months. Was it the stress of the job or the marital problems between himself and Sherry that caused him to cheat? He couldn't say, didn't really have time to figure it out. He used her and she him; the job she had as a secretary, he'd pulled those strings, purchased baubles and trinkets for her. He just considered cheating a diversion of sorts. Initially, it was the excitement of sneaking around and sex. But now even that was becoming old and he knew that he would soon break the whole thing off. The lies were getting harder to keep in line. He would be the first to admit that when he came here he didn't have to worry about cases he hadn't closed or being accused of not listening to his wife. In some ways it was as free as he had ever felt, until he prepared to go home, and that's when it hit him. If it wasn't for lying, adultery wouldn't be half bad.

He lied to Virginia, to Sherry, to himself. As a cop, he found lies to be an indispensable weapon in his arsenal of righteousness. When interrogating a suspect, he discovered, oftentimes you had to lie in order to get to the truth. And there was nothing more effective than a true lie. Lying was becoming comfortable as his favorite bathrobe, and that was bugging the hell out of him. Whenever he left from between Virginia's legs, he felt like a shell of a man, vacuous and transparent, and vowed that this would be the last time. But the emptiness persisted like a nagging toothache, and he found himself returning to rid himself of the pain, filling the void at the same time. He cared for Virginia and he appreciated her not always asking about police work, this case or that one, whenever they talked. She wasn't the prettiest or the smartest woman he'd ever met, but one thing he could say about Virginia— she never demanded anything of him. How much longer would the relationship go on? Somewhere between a day and for ever, Walter thought. But he knew that a time would come when the affair would have to end. Maybe she would find someone else and initiate the breakup with him. But he hoped not just yet. The very thought created a sense of longing and caused him to miss Virginia already.

Gunshots outside reminded Walter that he was a cop; sounded like the report of a .38. He had to catch a killer, somehow prevent his nephew from starting a blood bath, and do something about those white boys that tried to kill his grandmother—what exactly he didn't know. So much to do in so little time. All these thoughts along with the last swallow of beer formed a thick white pillow that slowly descended upon his head, suffocating him with sleep.

Working late, staying on top of things, my ass. Sherry Robinson rolled over, used her pillow for a punching bag. She rolled over again and pulled herself up in the bed, resting her back against the headboard. A combination clock and radio glowed on a bedside table; it was 2 a.m. She flicked on a lamp and picked up a paperback novel she'd left on the table, unfolded a dog-eared page and tried to read. She'd spent too many nights reading. Or pretending to. What does it matter anyway? Whether Walter is here or not, I'm always alone. There had been a time when she worried that the phone would ring in the middle of the night or that fellow officers would knock on her door with the foreordained news. From the beginning she was always Mrs Walter Robinson. Devoted, unassuming, self-effacing wife of a cop. She had sacrificed the dreams of continuing her education and college professorship to stay at home and see the world through the eyes of her husband. But breathing became difficult, the fabricated smiles transparent, and the ennui unbearable. She felt as though the walls of that fantasy were closing in upon her and that life was dehydrating one drop at a time. This was the dawn of a new millennium; it wasn't natural for a woman not to attempt to have it all. She found employment as Director of Public Relations with the local chamber of commerce, picking up the scent of her dreams and following them through evening courses at a local university, in pursuit of a master's degree. While that gave her a sense of self-fulfillment, it only increased the space between herself and Walter. Whatever she accomplished, he was never there to share it with. Not mentally anyway. The only thing worse than the space between them was the silence.

Sherry closed the book, sat with her arms folded, closed her eyes.

But it hadn't always been that way; things seemed to happen in stages. When she left Illinois to attend Tennessee State University, they'd met as juniors and were inseparable. Her parents thought Walter was nice enough alright, but a little too arrogant. If he wanted to start his own business, Chicago offered a lot more opportunities and their baby girl would be back at home. Who in hell ever heard of Forrest, Tennessee, anyway? Against their wishes she vowed everlasting love, slipped into his last name, then jetted to the Bahamas for a week of sunshine and consummation. His dreams of owning his own auto dealership began to fade from the frustration of too many closed doors. On a dare he took an entrance exam to the police academy, his marks so impressive that they literally dragged him through the front door. She could tell by the light in his eyes that he enjoyed going to work every day, the challenges that the job provided, status in the community. And she adjusted to the slower pace of small-town life. They had a reverence for the act of living and made plans for procreation. But after a few years on the force, things changed, he changed, and she guessed she did too. Everything, even a Sunday afternoon in the park, was viewed with a cynical eye, to be dissected and analyzed, every suggestion was camouflage for ulterior motives. Never a regular churchgoer, Walter rarely attended now, and she ventured again, alone. His moods vacillated like a needle on the barometer of emotion. Withdrawn, sullen, taciturn. Once, every so often, when she raised the notion about having a baby it was like lighting a match to a stick of dynamite. He ranted that he'd seen enough death, or worse, near-death, and he'd be damned if he would engage in cruel and unusual punishment by giving another Black child to this world. It was like he loved and hated the job at the same time. She knew he was out right now, turning over every rock in looking for his grandmother's attackers; she knew that if he got the chance he would kill them all without hesitation. Sherry hadn't broached the subject of having kids in years now. But she had to tell him now. He was still her husband and he had a right to know before he found out from someone else. She was five weeks pregnant. She had had plans to tell him this weekend but all hell broke loose with Big Mama and he had enough to worry about.

Sherry's heart skipped a beat in terror; her eyes opened wide from the shock of a solitary thought: would she feel remorse if her husband never came home again? Would she feel anything at all? The possible answers to the questions didn't horrify her as much as the mere questions themselves. She was afraid to delve within herself any farther to find out how she really felt. All she wanted was for her husband to listen to her. She would trade this house, the designer clothes, the BMW, and the jewelry if only he would listen. When they did talk, he anticipated, psychoanalyzed, took for granted her next thought pattern. She felt marginalized, as though she were undergoing interrogation in "the tomb" with the great Walter Robinson. Instead, she wanted him to hang upon her every word the way he did when they were first married, when words meant something. Now words were hollow shells of themselves, producing echoes of loneliness and remembrance before being tossed carelessly aside. She tried to imagine how he would react to learning he was going to be a father, the anger, distrust, disbelief. But it really didn't matter. She had feelings of her own to consider and having children was one of them. Being thirty-eight years old narrowed the years of opportunity for fertilization, and she wasn't going to do anything now to change what had happened; she anticipated that aspect of Walter's reaction also. She knew that if she didn't have this baby she would never have any, and she didn't want to be a bitter, regretful, resentful, irascible old woman before her time.

She laid the book on the bedside table, flipped off the light. She'd suggested marriage counseling, retreats to remedy their problems, and received broken promises instead. Sherry had come to understand that the only thing worse than a miserable marriage was a hypocritical one. What was the point of fabricating happiness in public when behind closed doors you had silent contempt for one another? The days were too short and dreams so fleeting. Something had to change. She'd come close to taking a lover, had flirted with Terrance Henderson, an attorney with his own practice. They'd lunched, shared suggestive phone calls, facial expressions. He'd made hotel arrangements and she'd agreed, but reneged, conflicted with impending guilt and the hope that things would get better between herself and Walter. But change was over the horizon of her mind like turbulent storm clouds and rain was inevitable. Whether the tempest produced a deluge or a sprinkling, the very air she breathed would carry a scent of freshness. Remaining the same in this place in this marriage in this life was like traveling a vast desert on a peripatetic course.

Sherry rolled onto her side, pulled the cover around her shoulders and tossed restlessly between sleep and vigilant anticipation of the moment her husband came through the door.

The man said he'd give him a hundred dollars. That's what the man said. All he had to do was bring in the rifle and that would be that. A Remington rifle. Easy money. Lee Sumner bounded down North Royal Avenue with a sense of purpose and mission. In his right hand he dangled a Remington hunting rifle draped in brown wrapping paper. Motorists and passers-by conferred curious looks, but he didn't notice. He tightened his grip around the neck of the barrel as he saw Lucky's pawn-shop a half-block away. The morning sun was rising like an omen in the eastern sky, threatening to consume the earth in conflagration. At 9 a.m. the day was already hot, producing rings of perspiration under Lee's arms, compelling him to wipe his brow with his shirtsleeve. But the walk in the heat was well worth it. Easy money, easy meth. It was a helluva lot better and safer to buy it than try to manufacture it yourself, Lee thought. He had had enough of that shit. If the police didn't raid the place and lock you up then you were likely, more than likely, to hurt yourself. Like the time he, Jamie, Ronny, and Tony, Ronny's brother, broke into an abandoned house and tried to cook their own batch of methamphetamine. Man, he got blamed for that, but he knew damn well Ronny put too much lighter fluid in the mix and literally blew the walls off the place. That was the closest they'd come to living on the edge and the thrill was exhilarating. They all laughed for weeks afterwards, counting themselves lucky that they escaped bodily injury, the police, and death; but he didn't find it funny when Ronny wisecracked to the other guys that it wasn't the excess lighter fluid that caused the explosion at all, but that's what happens every time fatass, meaning him, farted. Goddam that Ronny! If Lee wasn't so afraid of him he would love him. Or maybe that's why he did love him. No matter what he did to impress Ronny, it just wasn't good enough. But wait till the guys see what he'd done now. He'd scored on his own, and Ronny would have to respect him and stop calling him fatass all the time. With Jamie it was different and the same. He knew Jamie and Ronny both used him. But Jamie's words were soft, enticing. No matter what he suggested, you felt you wanted to do it and ended up doing it without realizing why. Ronny ranted and raved and backed it with the force of his fists. His weapons of motivation were fear and intimidation. Of the two, Lee admired Ronny. He knew that if Jamie couldn't talk him into something, that was the end of it. But with Ronny if hollering and screaming didn't work, he convinced you by beating the hell out of you. Didn't he shoot an old woman, twice, for nothing? Thought he killed her, but he didn't. Who couldn't admire a guy like that? He missed both of those guys, and didn't know where the hell either of them were right now. Just because they had a little falling out, so what? They'd argued and fought before. And they could make up and start all over again. But hell, it wouldn't be right for him to use all of the meth by himself.

The more excited Lee grew with his anticipated new

status the lighter his footsteps became, until it seemed as if he'd floated towards Lucky's and been lowered outside its front door after a bumpy landing. He used his hand to shield his eyes and leaned against the front glass, noticing the serenity of the scene, save for James 'Lucky' McCarthie perched on a stool behind the counter. Lucky was in an undershirt with a gold Rolex watch on his left wrist. His hairy arms and chest matched the fullness of his red beard. His lips moved as if he were talking to himself while being preoccupied with a newspaper on the counter before him, until he looked up, spotting Lee Sumner squinting through his plate-glass door.

Lee mopped his brow again, walked through the front door. "Hey, Mr Lucky."

Lucky folded the paper and pushed it aside. "C'mon in, son."

He approached the counter, full of smiles and expectation. Easy money, easy meth. "I got the rifle right here."

As soon as he laid the weapon down, an officer sprang from the floor behind the counter and leveled an assault rifle right between Lee's eyes. And from both sides of him materialized more cops with guns, all screaming in one voice distinct directives that froze Lee with confusion and fear, causing him to urinate upon himself in the middle of the floor.

Goddam! When Walter Robinson awoke it was eight o'clock Tuesday morning. He bolted upright, fumbled around in bed like a blind man groping for light. He sat on the side of the bed holding his head in his hands. His mind told him to jump up and get dressed, but his body felt lassoed by cords of lassitude. He called Virginia's name, his voice spreading in echoes throughout the house, bounding back upstairs, dying at his feet. He garnered strength to push himself off the bed. Virginia had left a note saying she hadn't woken him this morning, couldn't as a matter of fact, that last night was great as usual, that coffee was on and she was late for work herself.

Who in hell wanted coffee in this heat? He headed for the shower and turned the dials wide open, scrubbing the rank odor of sex and dried sperm down the drain. He would change clothes at home.

Minutes later, refreshed, he secured Virginia's house, picked his cell phone off the floor and went out the door. It was seventy-five degrees already when he put the car in drive, rolled down the windows, and slipped on his shades —the world slowing, becoming not so excessive. His phone rang with such force that it startled him.

"Robinson," he shouted into the mouthpiece.

"Walt? You alright?"

"Yeah, Hardegree. What's going on?"

"I got a couple of things. One, I talked to Telissa's mom and she said we're looking for the wrong boyfriend. Said that Telissa and Witherspoon were in love; he would never hurt her daughter. Said it's the new boyfriend, a Cornell Cox, that we should be tracking down."

"What she say about the knife incident between Witherspoon and Telissa?"

"She said that was just a heat-of-the-moment thing, the way lovers act sometimes. But she said Cox was a mean little bastard who studied evil. I ran a check on him also and he has a record dating back to when he was an embryo. Lot of assaults."

"Studied evil, huh?"

"What she said. Listen, Walt. I called your house around a hour ago and Sherry said you hadn't showed all night. Is everything OK? You sound hungover."

"I survived." He switched the phone from his left ear to his right, turning onto Perkins. "What's the other thing, Joe?"

"The city's in a panic, Walt. That fax was leaked to the press and this whole thing's about to explode. All our cops are anxious as hell. Some been calling in sick, others have sent their families away until this thing blows and the rest are carrying five or six weapons, including a knife or two. We got white women staying home from work and school fearing that they'll be the victim of some attack and white men saying this is the start of the race war and Black folks encouraging other Blacks to buy guns and a lot of ammo. Every available officer is on duty today."

Walter's thoughts were outrunning the ability of his tongue to form words, causing shortness of breath. Cebo. "I'll be damned. Any incidents?"

Joe coughed to clear his throat. "Lot of false alarms, man. And that asshole of a mayor we've got wants to call out the National Guard. Can you believe that? It's gonna be a helluva day. You on your way in?"

"I'll be there. In the meantime, pick up Cox and let's see if he's passed the course in evil. OK?"

"The SWAT team is banging on Cox's door as we speak."

"Good. Hey, Joe. Do me a favor?" Walter hesitated as if he couldn't find the words to say what he wanted to say. "Where are you now?"

"Just dropped a couple shirts off at the cleaners. I'm headed to the station, but I want to run by Telissa's crime scene one more time to make sure we didn't miss anything. What do you need, Walt?"

"Just be careful, willya?"

As he drove home, the city was like a rubber band stretched to breaking point. At any second the tension could snap, flooding the city with the lowest common denominator of human nature. The faces of passers-by and motorists were twisted into grimaces or contorted from confusion or bore blank stares of indifference. He could feel the thickness of anxiety in the air, sticky, lush, ponderous, making breathing difficult. The talk radio station filled the airwaves with threats, promises, warnings, *I-told-you-so*s, and curses in redneck drawls and Black militant bombast.

Exiting the bypass, entering his subdivision, Walter noticed how cool and clean the air had become, that kids still played, adults jogged, and that butterflies could be seen praying upon the altar of nectar. It was as though this section of the city was immune to what was transpiring only miles away. Jay Davenport, his neighbor, waved, backing out of his driveway for his morning commute to the office. Pulling into his own driveway, Walter killed the ignition and sat motionless behind the wheel. A sense of loneliness, terrible and immeasurable, came over him like a fever. He felt as though he belonged to nothing and was detached from everything. With clarity, for the first time, he began to see things as they were.

The suburbs. The name itself should have engendered magical feats like the words "hocus pocus" on the lips of a prestidigitator. Illusions of happiness, security, success, behind iron bars of gated communities with immaculate lawns and an SUV in every driveway. Each house cookie-cutter fashion with barbecues and homeowner's agreements. The good life built upon the accumulation of things and more things, paying tithes to the God of materialism until self-worth becomes measured in things. It was as though, Walter thought, an amorphous blob was chasing him and his neighbors through the streets of America, the blob being denial about the truth of past deeds and present realities. There were plenty of places to run but not very many to hide, and precious little time for either of them. Now Walter was on the run too, swept along and caught up beyond his control, looking over his shoulder every few seconds to see what if anything was about to overtake him, not knowing whether to scream out of fear or desperation. 'What am I doing here?' rang in his ears like sharp peals from a bell tower. He was a cop, and he never felt so comfortable as when he was chasing down leads and suspects and in the squad room and the tomb. Those were the things that had come to give fulfillment to his life; everything else had become artificial, hollow, meaningless diversions that he tripped over on his way to work every day. To his surprise, he found the front door unlocked, walked down the hall and stood upon the threshold of his bedroom. Through the half-opened door, he saw Sherry pulling clothes from the hangers of closet racks, tossing them on the bed.

"Hey," he stepped into the room, pulling his shirt off in the process, "you taking all that stuff to the cleaners? I thought you were taking off work until Big Mama got better?"

Sherry went back into the walk-in closet as though Walter hadn't ever been born.

"Sherry?" He followed her as she continued to arrange and rearrange. "How is Big Mama?"

She brushed past him throwing hatboxes on the bed. "I'm leaving you."

Like skywriting from a small engine plane, it took the words several seconds to solidify across Walter's mind. He laid his shirt on the back of a chair, impeded her path, looked deeply into his wife's eyes.

"What?"

"Feels like I'm dying. You have to choose between me or your whore. I can't take any more."

"Whore?" He had begun searching his mind for quick responses, testing his words for explanations regarding Virginia. "What in hell are you talking about, whore?"

"I'm talking about that goddam job! That's what I'm talking about."

Walter released a sigh anchored in relief.

"Wait a minute, Sherry…" He tried to grab her by the arm, but she pulled away from his grip and went back into the closet.

"No." She kept her back to him, gathering garments.

"There's nothing to wait for. I've waited for the marriage to get better. I've waited for you to care about the marriage getting better, and for the last time. I've waited for you to come home at eight in the morning for the last time. You're so busy keeping the world safe from crime that you don't even have time to go visit your grandmother lying in the hospital dying." She dropped more clothing onto the pile.

He put both hands on her shoulders. "Dying? You said she was showing signs of life."

"What's your problem?"

"I can't go by there and see her like that. I just can't." She tried to move and he refused to let her. "What in hell has gotten into you? Leaving me?"

"Yes. Leaving you." Her face was as placid as controlled anger. "I've tried everything I know to make this marriage work and you've tried everything to not make it work. Why should I or we be in a situation where neither one of us is happy? The time for faking it is over."

"Happiness? What's that?"

"Listen," she pointed her finger inches from his nose, "that's another thing. Don't give me any more of that philosophical bullshit. Save it for your partner. You talk to me like I'm your wife, at least for now anyway."

"OK. I'll change the way I talk to you. Is that what this is all about, changing me? Damn!" He turned, walked, confronted her from a few feet away. "I'm thirty-eight years old. Why would you even want to change me or anybody else for that matter?"

Sherry stepped over to where he was. "God almighty couldn't change you, Walter Lewis Robinson. And that's the last thing I want to do. All I ever wanted was for us to grow together, to share and bond with one another. I think they call that a family. But you're in a relationship with yourself and nobody can get through to you, except for the Forrest Police Department."

"How can you say I've never been here for you, Sherry?"

"Earlier, yes. But what about the last few years? Where were you last night?"

"Working. Uh, in case you've been living in a cave or something, the city is on the verge of a race war and if you've forgotten my grandmother was attacked and the assholes are out there still on the loose."

"And it's your job to hunt 'em down like dogs, even at the expense of your marriage?"

Walter put both hands on his hips, expelled a breath of frustration. "What the hell is it, Sherry? What do you want from me?"

"What do you want from yourself, Walter?" She matched his intensity step for step. "That's what I want to know. What do you want? I already know what I want. I found it over the years that we were together and I was alone. I've found me. And I found that I can stand on my own and survive on my own if I have to. Did you ever think about that? That I have dreams and goals too?"

"You want me to quit my job? Is that it?"

"No. Don't make yourself more miserable on my account."

"Your account? That's your problem right there, always has been the problem. You're the center of the universe. You wanna remove the splinter out of my eye when you got a two-by-four in your own."

"Oh, that is so cheap. Throw it all back on me the way

you always do. And we're quoting the Bible now, Walter?"

"Nah, we ain't quoting shit. I'm saying what I'm saying. You haven't been perfect in the marriage either, Sherry. You think you've been easy to live with? You're always right. Always gotta have things your way. You nag me over the smallest shit and you don't know when to let up. I'm who I am, imperfections and all. But you're always little Miss Perfect."

"Well, add one more to the list."

He hung upon the silence of her last word, waiting for her to fill in the blank.

"Pregnant." She turned from him, haphazardly stuffing suitcases.

Walter felt like a man waking from an anesthetic, drifting between dream and reality. "You're pregnant? You're carrying my baby? Sherry, talk to me, goddammit!"

Her words, laden with venom, uncoiled and sprang at him from across the room. "Oh, so now you want to talk. You bastard! I've already said all I need to say. I'm leaving and that's that."

"I thought we agreed not to bring another life into the suffering and misery of this world?"

"No. There was never an agreement. That was your declaration. Well, guess what? You changed, I changed. I wasn't trying to get pregnant, never thought I would, but things change." She started to leave the room, suitcases in both hands.

"Hold up, Sherry." Walter grabbed her by the biceps, spun her around. "How can we throw everything away like this? We can work this thing out." His voice dropped in volume and tone.

Sherry evaded his grasp, paused on the threshold of the bedroom. "Do you want to work it out, Walter?"

"If I didn't I would be helping you carry your bags right now," he said, pronouncing each word as if he were taking a final breath. "What in hell do you think I want to do, Sherry? You just told me I'm about to be a father, for Christ's sake."

They stared at one another over the expanse of years they'd shared together and recognized one another for the first time in a very long time. "Well, I need some space right now to work some things out with myself," she said, choking back tears with the words. "I'll be over Marcia's house."

"Hey." Walter stopped her a final time. "When was the last time we made love?"

All of the blood shot to Sherry's head. "Meaning?" She could see a wheel of questions spinning in Walter's mind. "Oh, you have doubts whether it's your baby, huh? Well, you can go straight to hell." She turned and didn't look back.

Walter looked around him. The bedroom was in disarray, with clothes strewn on the floor and the bed unmade; even the morning sun streaming through the windows cast slovenly shadows on the wall. The sound of Sherry closing the front door behind her was like that of a cell door slamming. The entirety of his thirty-eight years of living was reduced to this one solitary moment upon this single spot in the middle of his bedroom floor. He walked into the closet, tripped over one of Sherry's shoes, grabbed pants, shirt, underwear, jacket and tie from the shelves. He looked at the clock on the dresser and realized that he was both late and running out of time.

Halfway to the precinct, he was thankful that his telephone rang, interrupting thoughts of Sherry walking out on him, his mind replaying the scene like a phonograph needle stuck in a vinyl groove.

"I'm on my way, Hardegree," he said, squeezing the phone between his shoulder and ear.

"Is this Detective Robinson?"

"Yeah. Who dis?"

"Lucas Witherspoon. I've been looking for you."

Walter moved the phone from one ear to the other. "No shit. I've been looking for you too. Where ya at? Stay there. I'm on my way."

He swung a U-turn and made a right onto Cooper, avoiding the bypass. At a stop light, he pulled up behind a late-model Ford pickup with two adults and a teenage boy between them. All three were dressed in hunting fatigues with orange caps, and over the teenager's head in the rear window hung a Remington rifle. Immediately, Walter heard the crunch of snapping twigs underfoot in the crispness of winter woods. He was a teenager with a Remington rifle slumped over his shoulder, trailing behind Uncle Melvin and Grandaddy Marshall like a wide-eyed, droopy-eared puppy dog. They were down in river-bottom land in the early morning hours shortly after daybreak, trying to entice a buck into the cross-hairs of high-powered rifles. Uncle Melvin, long, lean, slow-footed and taciturn, kept a half-pint in his back pocket for hunting excursions; most things he had to say, except for an occasional grunt of approval, came from the barrel of a gun. Grandaddy, every movement closely calculated, had a meticulously trimmed mustache that he nervously groomed with his fingers and piercing black eyes that penetrated into the past, gleaning timeless wisdom for future possibilities. Each of his seventy years upon the planet possessed a life lesson. When Walter first moved to the country he begged and begged his grandaddy to teach him how to swim. Finally, Grandaddy relented and took him down to the pond with instructions to jump in, kick his feet as fast as possible, bring his elbows out of the water with each stroke, and, oh yeah…don't forget to breathe. It was usually that way with most things Walter sought advice on, from fixing the tractor to milking a cow, all instructions ending with the maxim: "If you can't do it right, don't do it at all." He was an endless reservoir of anecdotes and aphorisms that revolved around unspoken words like knowledge, diligence, and commitment. Like when waiting for hours camouflaged against the hillside anticipating a ten-point buck strolling into the clearing. They had scouted, chosen the perfect location behind a clump of shrubbery, and, lying prone on their bellies, had a view of the world through two bare branches.

"Let me tell you something, boy," Grandaddy Marshall advised him. "How old are you now? Fifteen? Well, you almost a man. You go out here and kill one of these crackers, you'll see what I'm talking about, and since you're almost a man you need to know something. Somebody always want you to do it the way they want you to do it. But you've got to learn to be your own self. Yes. Take good advice, but in the end you're the one that's gonna have to live or die with what you done chose. You ain't gonna always have me or your grandmama to hold your hand. One day you gonna look around and all there's gonna be is you. Guess what? We didn't bring you hunting. You brought us out here." Grandaddy Marshall pushed himself up from the ground while Uncle Melvin followed suit, dropping a half-pint on the ground beside Walter, and they both scampered off through the brush.

This was a helluva Christmas present. A Remington rifle and being tossed to the woods. He shivered with each change of direction in the wind, the ground beneath him feeling like a block of ice. Yet he continued staying alert to every sound, looking down the barrel of his gun into the clearing, staying attentive, quiet, and unwavering, like a guard at Buckingham Palace; he imagined, or hoped anyway, that Grandaddy Marshall and Uncle Melvin were near by observing his every action and probably laughing their asses off. Walter removed a handkerchief from his breast pocket, wiped his nose, replaced it. He picked up the flask Uncle Melvin had left behind, unscrewed the cap, drank. His body was tangled in a spasm of coughs, and when he shook himself free, a bitter warmness spread through his veins like encroaching shadows at dusk. He wasn't as cold as before and the world, momentarily anyway, had become lucid around the edges.

He filled the passing hours with thinking of how he would brag to his buddies about how many deer he'd bagged, how much whiskey he'd drank, and all the talk he, his uncle, and grandfather shared about women. On several occasions he could've pulled the trigger on a doe or two, but that would've made him look like a pussy in front of the fellows, not being able to kill a buck like a man. As ten o'clock approached, the air began to warm, thawing the earth beneath him, and he was resigned to killing a doe and dancing to the music of puerile persecution. Then, like the fin of a killer shark protruding off a tropical coast, a set of twelve-point antlers emerged, and Walter anticipated hearing music in surround sound warning that something bad was about to happen. The buck hesitated at the edge of the clearing, his gait regal, his crown majestic, sniffed, pawed, moved forward.

Walter began to shake uncontrollably, his excitement barely allowing him to load, raise his rifle at the deer. He felt as if he were peeping through a keyhole into the bedroom of a naked woman. The buck was stunning! He had to constantly remind himself to calm down, especially now that the buck was looking directly at him, the gaze of his enormous round eyes like black lasers powerful enough to split trees in half. This may have been his first hunt alone, but he had been on several hunts vicariously. He'd heard his grandfather recount several times how he had shot a buck this way and that way, and Walter knew, even though he had a clear shot, to wait until the buck presented him with a target right between the ribs. But if he waited a second too long the buck would pick up his scent and that would be that. Thanks a lot, Grandaddy Marshall and Uncle Melvin. Ever heard of a tree stand?

The buck became distracted by a sound to his right, turning his head (what a beautiful profile), and for a moment Walter thought that he was going to flee in the opposite direction. But he lowered his head, gleaning the ground for food, moving farther into the clearing with each mastication. Walter measured his target, the spot between the shoulder and the final rib, felt the springs of the trigger give under the weight of his finger and then watched the trees as they swayed from the blast of his exploding rifle. The buck jumped four feet as if the earth were a trampoline, was suspended spreadeagle in mid-air, then hit the ground in a full sprint. Walter rejoiced in the shot with several celebratory yells and an improvised dance. He looked behind him, calling for Grandaddy Marshall and Uncle Melvin, and when they didn't emerge, followed, rifle in hand, after the wounded animal. He picked up a blood trail that led thirty yards into the woods, and ten yards away lay the buck collapsed on his right side. Walter approached, the leaves crunching beneath his feet, and treated the buck like a rattlesnake, poking him from a distance with the barrel of his gun. He kneeled, dropped the gun on the ground, inspected the gaping hole in the buck's side, its blood forming a pool on the black, bitter earth. He could feel the presence of someone moving behind him and could just see the smiles of approbation upon his kinfolk's faces. When he stood and turned, his own smile landed upon his shoelaces. Walter was staring into the bared teeth of a coyote. The coyote was in attack stance, mangy, rabid, ravenous, saliva drooling from the mouth. There were two textbook alternatives: flight or fight. Four legs were always faster than two, but he'd just killed a twelve-point buck like a natural man and just didn't feel like running. Walter knew that, with the rifle behind him, by the time he reached around to grab the weapon the coyote would be upon his throat. But that was a chance he had resigned himself to. He took a step backwards, feeling for the gun with his right foot, and once upon it stooped to grab, aim, and fire. But his balance became lost between thought and deed and before he knew it he was flat on his back with no weapon at all and the bared teeth of a mad coyote charging at him. His last option was to sacrifice his left arm to the coyote's teeth, hoping to buy time for his right hand to find a rock in the vicinity.

Walter didn't see anything, only heard the growl of the coyote and the echoes of a gunshot. He opened his eyes, rose up on his elbows and saw Uncle Melvin walking towards him with a smoldering rifle in his hand.

"Where my liquor at, boy?" Uncle Melvin towered over him, offered Walter his right hand.

"Man," he dusted dirt and debris from his clothes. "I'm glad to see ya'll. I thought I was gonna have to break that damn coyote's neck."

Grandaddy Marshall walked up and surveyed the scene around them. He removed his cap, shook his head, flipped the cap back on. "Goddam, boy. You tried to kill all the animals in the woods, didn't ya?" He nudged Uncle Melvin in the ribs, patted his grandson on the back. "Look at the size of that buck, will ya? Ain't nothing like barbecue deer. Lets load 'em up."

The three of them dragged the buck to a pickup truck and hefted him in the back. Walter sat in the middle between his uncle and grandfather with a Remington rifle above his head. Occasionally, he turned and looked back and felt an overwhelming sense of lament at seeing the big, black, doleful eyes of the lifeless deer. Strangely, he wished the deer still alive. Such a magnificent animal, its beauty found in the freedom of its legs. But there is no beauty in anything dead. He wished the deer had never come into the clearing, had chosen another part of the woods to traverse, wished the rifle had jammed, anything. Within a split second the deer ceased to be a deer and what had become of him, Walter? It had been another day of seeking food and water, and death, like the chill of a winter morning, had crept up on the both of them. Now they both were the hunted. Only the deer was like an aborted dream, now never to run gracefully through woods and streams, leaving Walter with lingering feelings of guilt and shame. Looking at the animal lying in the bed of the truck, Walter felt a sense of finality. A second later and he would've been riding in the back of the truck and a coyote would've been looking down from a hillside, recalling the taste of human blood. Death is always reduced to fractions of seconds and life is lived in the space between. What would tomorrow mean for him? Would it be the last day of his fifteen-year-old life or the first minute of a childhood memory? Walter took a final look out of the rear window and jumped when the buck winked an eye at him.

The blaring of horns, angry and impatient, could be heard from a stream of cars behind Walter Robinson, causing his daydream to evaporate like boiling water. He waved in his rearview mirror and accelerated through a green light.

"Where's your mama?" Walter stood in the doorway of Lucas Witherspoon's apartment. He was dressed in undershirt, short khaki pants, sandals. He smelled of soap from a hot shower, cheap cologne. "You eat pig's feet?"

"No, sir. If it ain't a vegetable or a fruit I don't fool with it. Mama? I don't know. Probably at the store. Come on in." After formal introductions they shook hands, sat at the kitchen table. "Can I get you something to drink?"

Walter pulled out a pad and pen from his shirt pocket. "No thanks. Just talk to me Lucas. Why did you cut Telissa?"

Lucas had his back to Walter, closing the door of the refrigerator after pouring himself a tall glass of carrot juice. He crawled over the back of the chair and settled opposite Walter at the table, shaking his head. "I don't know. That was three years ago. You know that, right? Anyway, I live with that every day now. It's not like I was trying to do it. We was living together at the time and had a fight, a bad fight. It started with hollering and screaming, then shoving and slapping, and then she went into the kitchen. When she came back down the hall she had a knife and came at me with it. We fought over that, too, and while I was wrestling her to the ground, she got cut and I got busted. Later, and I ain't telling you nothing new, she dropped the charges."

"I don't care if it was three years or three minutes ago. Why y'all break up? Cause of the fight?"

Lucas's arms and chest were evidence of countless hours spent in weight rooms and health spas. His muscles were well defined, and with his closely cropped haircut and clean-shaven face he could've passed for a letterman on a football team at any local college. He swallowed half the juice, stirred the rest in concentric circles with a flick of his wrist.

"Nah. If anything the fight brought us closer together, for a while anyway. We was just moving in different directions, Detective Robinson. I'm a factory worker, been punching a time clock for twelve years. That's all I know. All of my dreams can be found in the four walls of that plant. It's steady and secure, right now anyway. But she wanted to go to school and do this and that. Like she was growing wings and I couldn't, didn't want to be the one to hold her down. Always talking about starting her own school and helping kids. I've never wanted nothing but the best for Telissa. Even if it meant letting her go." He brought the glass to his mouth again, leaving a wet ring on the table.

Walter looked up from his note-taking. "When was the last time you saw her? Alive."

"Uh, 'bout two weeks ago. It was her birthday and I took a present by the house."

Walter cleared his throat. "Were the two of you still sleeping together?"

"No. We came close. But she said she never cheated on me and she wasn't going to cheat on her new boyfriend either."

There was a long pause, and in the silence Lucas's face became taut like the skin of a drum, eyes clouded with wetness, voice strained. "A ruby bracelet."

"What?" Walter looked up.

"I gave her a ruby bracelet for her birthday."

In the interval of quiet that fell upon the room, only the scratching of Walter's pen could be heard saturating the silence. He looked up just as the sun darted behind clouds, filling the room with the shadow of light. The small kitchen was fractured by tone variations; the table, chairs, sink, cupboards, stove, floors, both he and Witherspoon, had been mutated by the shadow of light. And he was tempted to go outside, where the world would await with the finality of a glare. There would be no tones, hues, or colors, just reality, butt ass naked in black and white. For the past couple of days he'd come to understand that the whole of his life had been lived in the shadow of light. He'd always been adept at divorcing his emotions from any situation, preserving a semblance of peace. But time had run its course, and now everything was tangled more than ever into the shadow of light. There were no colors to hide behind. Only two variations of the spectrum to deal with whether he wanted to or not. His life was holding up a mirror for him to draw his own judgments. After thirty-eight years, the question should have been settled years ago, and he thought it had been. But he'd found ways of deluding himself about who he was and what it meant to be him. Big Mama, his wife, white boys, race riots, his nephew, the job—all of it was a swirling force of wind, rain, and earth revolving around his life. Life. It's a helluva thing. We're born, we die, and the space in between is spent trying to figure out who we are and how we came to be and why we are and where we're going and what in hell we're going to do when we get to where it is we think we should be and how none of that is never enough, stumbling along a path illuminated by a shadow of light. We seek money, happiness, fame, power, and glory as imperfect beings in imperfect places in an imperfect world, and receive temporary fulfillment and constant rays from the shadow of light. Thirsting for freedom, love, beauty, and peace in mountaintop experiences, we cry out for a deluge of understanding, receiving instead only a few drops from the valley of the shadow of light.

Walter felt his heart constrict from skipping several beats. From many years ago, a phrase he'd learned in Sunday School, "through a glass darkly," came to his mind. He tried to remember, quote the scripture in its entirety, but couldn't. It's a helluva thing. And it's a shame, Walter thought, I guess you have to die to find out what life is truly all about. He thought of these things often, and could have done so all day today. Instead, he closed his notepad, realizing that Lucas Witherspoon was innocent from the get-go. Witherspoon's breathing was easy and measured, his body language didn't contradict his words, and there wasn't the scent of anxiety oozing from his pores. But most of all there were his eyes. Placid, direct, brown. He, Walter, had developed over the years the ability to peer into the eyes of a suspect and unveil the truth at the heart of intent and meaning. He checked his watch, realizing he should be at the station by now, threw out perfunctory questions.

"Where were you two nights ago?"

Lucas drifted out of his daze as if he heard someone calling his name from a distance of hills and valleys. "Uh…" He dropped his head, rubbed his forehead. "Uh… working—"

"You work every night?"

"I was working." He looked Walter directly in the eye. "You can check with my supervisor and co-workers."

"I'll do that." Walter rested his chin in his hand, elbow on table. He stuffed his notepad and pen inside his shirt. "I think I will have a glass of water. If you don't mind?"

Lucas rattled ice in a glass, filled it to the rim from the spigot.

"So. You got any ideas who would want Telissa dead?"

Lucas pushed the glass beneath Walter's nose, slid back into the seat with his legs alongside the table, crossed at the knee. "Yeah. That little motherfucker."

"I know several little motherfuckers. Which one in particular?"

He raised his eyebrows, bringing the glass to his lips.

Witherspoon looked into the distance, replaying images upon the big screen of his mind. "I should've beat 'im down when I had the chance. The little motherfucker I'm talking about is Cornell Cox. Telissa and I bumped into one another coming out of a movie one night and the little bastard slings her up against the wall and steps up to me, talking a whole lotta shit. But he's a straight-up coward, Detective Robinson. I told him I'd meet 'im outside, but he just kept hollerin' and screaming at Telissa. He never showed." Witherspoon shook his head, as if experiencing a realization for the first time. "When I think about it Telissa was just a good ass-kicking from being alive."

"Maybe. Maybe not." Walter finished his drink. "After you had kicked his ass, he probably would've come back with some of his boys for the payback. You said he was a coward, right? That's what cowards do."

"It doesn't matter. My life for Telissa's is more than an even swap. I understand that we don't have a choice when it comes to dying. But what we're willing to die for, hell, that's all up to us."

Walter set the glass aside, pushed himself up from the chair. The sun shifted beyond the clouds, filling the kitchen with warm, brilliant, yellow light. "Thanks for the water. And for giving me a call. Hell, you tracked me down. And don't break town no time soon." He extended his hand to Witherspoon.

Lucas pumped Walter's hand twice. "You don't have to worry about that. That goddam factory has papers on me. If there's anything I can do to help, holler at me." He continued to hold the officer's hand. "I'm sorry to hear about your grandmother."

Puzzled, Walter asked, "How you know about that?"

"This is Forrest, Tennessee." Witherspoon smiled. "Everybody knows everybody's business here. Or think they do anyway."

Walter pulled his hand away and said goodbye.

"Peace, brother."

Waiting for the light to change at the intersection of Royal and Jackson, Ronny McAlister knew it was on. Directly across from him was a black-and-white cruiser and the officer was looking him over like a choice piece of meat in a butcher's shop window. Driving the most wanted stolen car in the country at 9 a.m. on a Tuesday morning was like having "arrest me" tattooed on your forehead. Ronny floored the gas pedal before the light changed to green, accelerating past the cop in a blur of screeching rubber and exhaust fumes. The officer switched on sirens and lights, shouted codes into the handset of his radio, executed a U-turn and started in pursuit. Ronny threw back his head and released a rebel yell. He cranked the radio as loud as it would go until the music was blurred static rattling the speakers of the Caprice Classic. The draft rushing through the windows brushed his ponytail into an upward motion. Goddam, this feels good! He sped through a red light, barely missing a black Mercedes SUV. The reason for his exhilaration was not running from the police. Instead, he was moving towards freedom. He had never felt this good about anything in all his life. There was nothing he couldn't do, nothing to stop him but space and wind.

Ronny felt as though he sat upon a rocket slicing through gravity and space, with the Big Dipper in plain sight. In one ear the engine of the '95 Chevrolet and in the other ear the sirens growing in intensity and proximity, exhorting him to go, man, go! Approaching the intersection of Lexington and Royal, he incessantly blew his horn, deftly driving onto the sidewalk and maneuvering around stalled traffic. This caused him to release from his throat a sound between laughter and a shout. He had been telling people all along that he was a man. Now he was *the* man. He controlled two tons of steel. He controlled the Forrest Police Department. He controlled the streets of a municipality. He controlled his life and his destiny. He didn't need any goddam body. Fuck Jamie, Lee. And his mother was dead to him now. He hoped he saw his always perfect brother crossing the street right now; he would squash him like a bug. And fatass? He's been going all over town trying to leave word for me that he was about to come into some money so they could score. Jamie? Who wanted the three of them to lay low? Fuck that. He was tired of taking bullshit orders from him.

And after the other night, he owed him an ass-kicking. It was just Ronny McAlister versus the world. Hadn't it always been that way? Well, now, look out. The world was in trouble.

Ronny raced through city streets at speeds in excess of 90 miles per hour. It gave him the sensation of taking a strong drink of whiskey. He swallowed again and again, trying to preserve that feeling of intoxication. He thought about the time he was twelve years old and took his first hit of methamphetamine. Man, he didn't think he'd ever come down and didn't want to. He was flying now and he hadn't taken anything all morning.

He blitzed another intersection, causing motorists to slam brakes, blow horns, and pump the air with angry fists and a myriad of invectives. There were just too many stop lights in this town. Something was always getting in his way, slowing him down. If I can just get onto the expressway, I'll lean out of this window and tell these motherfuckers to kiss my ass, Ronny thought to himself as he approached the intersection Royal and Chippewa.

Cebo could spot a cop from a mile away, a few yards across a parking lot, or driving down a major city street at nine o'clock in the morning. They way they dressed, walked, talked, and smelled simply had to be standard issue, along with their badge and revolver. Besides, he knew this blue-eyed, blond-headed guy, coming out of the dry cleaners with a cell phone glued to his ear, entering a vehicle, was a cop. He had pulled Cebo over for a busted taillight, ordered him out of the vehicle and arrested him for a couple marijuana cigarettes in the ashtray three years ago.

Cebo whipped his Jeep across two lanes of oncoming traffic onto a side street, turned the vehicle around, parked with the engine humming. He rolled down his tinted window. From where he sat, he had an unobstructed view of Forrest's finest fastening his seatbelt, putting his blue Dodge Intrepid in reverse. Halfway between cloud and sun, the day was thick and muggy, the air stirred occasionally by a slight breeze as a portent of rain. Cebo's shirt wanted to stick to his body, his hands began to sweat; he readjusted his baseball cap out of habit.

"What's this?" Jook was in the passenger seat, recovering from the sudden stunt car maneuver and a possible whiplash. He had been an Apostle for three years and had moved quickly up through the ranks exhibiting altruistic attitudes and committing acts of fidelity. Cebo knew that, as long as there were members like Jook, the organization would always be around.

"Hold tight." Cebo watched the officer look both ways before merging into traffic. "Get the bitch out the back."

Jook hopped out of the vehicle, retrieved an assault rifle from its rear and re-entered with a single bound. His breaths came in rapid succession and, laying the weapon across his lap, he was wide eyed with excitement, grinning a mouthful of gold.

He looked from Cebo to the weapon and back to Cebo. "Gotdam, dogg! This the baddest thang I've ever seen. I've been dreaming about one of these all my life. She's beautiful!" Jook made sure the safety was on, pointed the weapon towards the windshield, spied an imaginary target through the scope, and beamed from ear to ear at the power he imagined the gun would bestow upon him. "She got much kick to her?"

"You'll fine out. Be patient." Cebo eyed Jook out of the corner of his eye, lowering the rifle below the dashboard with his free hand. "Easy, man. It's got your name on it."

Cebo fell into traffic behind a white bread truck with red lettering, two vehicles behind the blue Intrepid. He wasn't worried about losing the chase. Over the years he'd become adroit at trailing someone unawares. Besides, the Intrepid had distinctive Vanderbilt University markings on its license plate. His primary concern was finding a spot where he could get a clean shot at his target and make an even cleaner getaway. Gas station, convenience store, post office—all of the above had been proved as ideal killing grounds. Jook realized that they were in pursuit of the blue Intrepid and hoped his patience would pay off soon.

The bread truck signaled, turned left onto Trailwood. Cebo changed lanes, tried to remain inconspicuous behind a grey Mercedes. A mile later, he noticed his nark with pen and paper in hand, using the steering wheel for support to scribble notes, before the light changed and traffic surged in a massive wave of steel and glass.

"What the hell *is* this?" Jook marveled, caressing the rifle from muzzle to sight to buttstock as if it had the long, curvaceous lines of a woman.

"AR-15. Colt," Cebo spat from the corner of his mouth, not taking his eyes off the road.

Jook was practically drooling. "Man, I think I like this better than the AK. This bitch look like she can't miss." Cebo knew well of Jook's affection for weaponry and if he would have kissed the gun it wouldn't have surprised him.

The longer they drove the fewer the stop lights, the thinner the traffic congestion and the more adept Cebo became at accelerating, changing lanes and slowing down so as not to draw attention to himself. Occasionally, in the throes of concentration, he would utter "Yeah" to Jook's inquiries or even when Jook said nothing at all, until he noticed that paved city streets were evolving into gravel country roads lined with the lushness of all things idyllic and pastoral.

Where in hell is this guy going? Without other cars on the road, Cebo drove five miles over the speed limit, using the distance between himself and the vehicle in front of him as camouflage to lower doubts and suspicions. Two thoughts wrestled for control in his mind. If his suspect was going out of town, to hell with it. He'd have to find another cop for another time. Around here, he knew places to hide and people to help him hide in those places. But to shoot a cop outside of the city limits and make it back to Forrest entailed too many variables beyond his control. He'd be hung out to dry upside down, butt naked and without a towel. But the more Cebo contemplated, the more the idea of pulling alongside the blue Intrepid, rolling down the window and allowing Jook to fire a couple of rounds began to take shape and solidify in his mind.

"Open that glove compartment," Cebo ordered, "and load one of those magazines. And roll your window down."

"What size ammo is this, dogg?" Jook loaded the weapon, poised to aim it out the window and fire.

".223."

Jook tightened an orange bandanna around his head.

"Gotdam! Tell you what, if we don't shoot this motherfucker, maybe we can find us an elephant out here in the woods somewhere. Guy probably got a better chance than the elephant." He laughed out loud, as if he were a standup comic amused at his own jokes.

Cebo stared him down, overpowered him with intensity. "Enough of that. Time to go to work. When I give you the signal…OK?"

It was now or never. There was no oncoming traffic or anyone riding his rear end, nothing but space and opportunity. He stomped upon the accelerator and thought he'd punched a hole through the floorboard, feeling the thrust of the engine beneath him and the pull of gravity upon his face.

The Intrepid had pulled to the side of the road and parked. What in the hell is this guy doing? Had they been spotted? Had he radioed for backup or was he mounting a counter-attack of his own?

To slam on the brakes now would spin the car out of control and careen it into a nearby ditch. Instead, Cebo continued a half-mile down the road, turned the car around in the first driveway he came to, and headed back towards the blue Intrepid.

He slowed the vehicle to a creep when the Intrepid was in sight, its emergency lights flashing like a plea from the side of the road. The cop had removed his jacket and was walking towards an open field, his head down like a bloodhound hot on a scent. Pulling to the side of the road a few yards down and opposite the Intrepid, Cebo left the vehicle in park with the engine humming. He and Jook sat silently until a late-model Buick came towards them, passed. Cebo checked his rearview mirror. Nobody. The sun darted from behind a bank of clouds and produced a shower of light, concentrated and brilliant.

With one hand Cebo rolled down his window and with the other grabbed the rifle from Jook, provoking a look of disappointment in his passenger. But this is the way it should be, Cebo thought. He had conceived this plan and with one shot he would be the one to bring it screaming into the world. He'd said forty-eight hours in the fax. But that was part of the plan too. Tell the bastards one thing and give 'em something else to keep 'em off balance. He'd learned a long time ago that the only way to deal with white folks, if you wanted to survive, was to lie to them. And this wasn't to be some random act of senseless violence for the hell of it or seeking a moment of fame; he'd seen and had enough of that. This was a political act. A statement of manhood. A declaration of courage. An outcry against injustice. A message of dignity. A eulogy to hopelessness. Proclamation for a new day.

All of the thoughts filtered from Cebo's mind to his left eye pressed against the sight of the rifle and to his index finger curled around the trigger. The cop was walking in irregular circles, combing the field with his vision, occasionally stooping to pick up an object, examining it before standing, tossing it aside. Cebo didn't know what the hell he was looking for, but he would never find it. At a hundred yards the cop's blond head was a ripe melon, and Cebo's vision was so clear he could read the designer's logo on the officer's button-down shirt.

Just breathe.

He counted seconds off in his head, coordinating

inhaling and exhaling with the moment he would squeeze the trigger. Cebo heard Jook's phone but it rang in desultory tones, as if it were halfway across the world; he didn't know whether he was hearing things or not.

"Yo, dogg! It's your girl." Jook's voice raised an octave in alarm.

Cebo flipped off the safety, fixed his mouth in a thin, determined line.

"Yo, dogg. It's Leslie." He covered the mouthpiece with his hand. "It's your uncle. He hurt."

Cebo blinked, emerged from a thick, heavy fog. "What?"

"He's hurt bad, man."

Cebo tossed the rifle onto the floor in the back and dropped the car into gear, tires scratching and screeching in an attempt to find traction on the road.

At the sound of burning rubber, the officer whipped around, ducked and drew his weapon from its holster. When he raised up, there was only the sight of taillights fading into the distance.

Halfway back into town, Cebo wondered who had fucked up. Nobody was to do any shooting until they'd heard from him. And most of all his uncle wasn't to be harmed in any way. He couldn't get the image of Big Mama lying in the hospital out of his mind, and now Uncle Walter hurt or maybe even worse. Who was responsible for this? What in the world happened?

At about the same time Cebo was stalking a Forrest police officer, Walter had just left Lucas Witherspoon's apartment and had phoned the station to see whether Detective Hardegree had made it in and had uncovered any new evidence from the crime scene. Hardegree wasn't in. But Lieutenant Peters informed him that Cornell Cox had been picked up and was awaiting questioning as they spoke, and speaking of which, where in hell were his two detectives who were supposed to be investigating the case? Walter asked about any incidents of racial strife developing into violence. Lieutenant Peters responded in the negative and ordered him to get his ass down there ASAP. Walter replied in the affirmative and hung up the phone.

Walter Robinson maneuvered the vehicle in the direction of Precinct Four and as was his habit flipped on WNES-FM to get his morning dose of news, weather, and moronic observations. It was as if he'd gone to sleep and woken three days later, or maybe he had been in a time warp, like someone wearing a polyester suit in 2007. There seemed only three topics of conversation everywhere he turned: his grandmother, gang bangers (Black thugs), and the impending race war (white supremacists). He cut the radio off, listened to the music of passing cars and buses and silence. He reached into the glove compartment, retrieved his revolver and two-way radio. He was old school. While the department's issued weapon was a .40 semi-automatic, he still opted for a .357 Magnum, his philosophy being that it ain't how many times it will shoot but how straight the person doing the shooting can aim it. Walter slid the revolver into his shoulder holster, the two-way radio slipping out of his hand. The radio hit the floor between his legs and came on, blaring snatches of a high-speed chase—white male, white Caprice Classic, suspect in an attempted homicide. Walter picked the radio up from the floor, increased the volume and, laying it on the seat next to him, turned the car from Preston onto Vance.

He pulled into a nearby parking lot and increased the volume on the radio even more, listening intently. Each word crawled from the radio's small speaker with a life of its own, like an occupying army invading foreign territory. MCP-439. Repeat. License number MCP-439. Royal and Chippewa. White male. White Caprice Classic. It was all a massive tidal wave rolling his way, fast and fierce, threatening to sweep him along into oblivion. His mind was racing against the current of events, thinking, plotting, contemplating what to do next, and it didn't take him long to figure it out. He jerked the car back into traffic and floored it down McCowat, rolled a stop sign headed for High View; from High View it was a straight shot to Chippewa. And when he reached Chippewa he gunned the engine down to where Chippewa intersected Royal. It wouldn't be long now. He had a clear view of all the traffic flowing freely down Royal Avenue. It was just a matter of time before the deer came into the clearing. Again, he pulled into the curb, checked his weapon, stuck his badge on his lapel pocket, adjusted the seatbelt and set the portable blue light on the roof of the car. He unfastened his seatbelt, reached over the back seat and retrieved his bullet-proof vest, then rebuckled. For the past forty-eight hours what in hell had he done? The answer came back, weighty with the sound of silence. He'd collected evidence, interviewed a suspect and still hadn't caught a killer. Talk, talk, talk. And listless talk at that; he couldn't even stop his wife from walking out on him. His grandmother would probably never be the same. Walter only hoped that all three of the sonofabitches were in the car. He was about to declare a personal jihad. Sacrificing his life wasn't much compared to making everything right. Big Mama, Sherry, Cebo, the guys on the force, his unborn child, would all remember him as either a martyr or a fool. But remembered nonetheless. Hell, he would even do the city a favor by averting a race war. He had an inexplicable sense of peace about him, as if he were in the presence of something divine. All of his years on the force had taught him to think analytically, but now, as a speeding white Chevrolet, his grandmother's Chevrolet, darted down Royal Avenue, he knew it was the end of intellectualism and that somebody had to die. He thought of scribbling a final note, hurriedly, but decided his actions would speak for themselves. He only wanted his child, male or female, to know that their daddy was a man who was not afraid to walk it like he talked it and that he loved them very much.

He heard the tumult of police cars in pursuit before he saw the white sedan falling off a hill, bearing down over his left shoulder. The Caprice Classic was moving at such a speed that Walter saw space between wheels and ground, the vehicle a pied piper trailing half the city's police department behind it, while in front of it motorists had scattered to the side of the road. He left his own vehicle in park, gunned the engine, and mumbled under his breath. In a few seconds, people would have nothing but good things to say about him, like they always do about the dead; he just hoped that he wouldn't maim anyone or take any innocent lives. He put the car in drive, held his foot on the brake for a fraction of a second longer, then stomped on the accelerator with all of his might. The rear wheels ignited and blazed, screaming for traction, before ejecting the car into the intersection. Walter struck the rear quarter panel as if it had a bull's-eye painted on it, causing a furore of twisted metal and smashing glass. The late-model Chevy spun twice clockwise, crashing into a yellow Buick waiting for the light to change twenty feet away.

Walter's initial response was to fight his way out of the white fog but halfway into unconsciousness he realized that this was part of the plan and decided to welcome death with surrender. But the more he resigned himself to the hereafter the more it felt like the right now; there were no concertos in B flat major or streets paved with gold and the bosom of God was an inflated airbag that he rested his head upon as the fog dissipated to the sound of someone's blaring horn superglued to the center of his brain. He shook the cobwebs from his mind, finding the hood of his car missing, steam shooting from the radiator, two tires flat, the front end halfway across town, recognized that he had been spun counterclockwise, that he was facing north on Royal when initially he hade been headed south. And he realized, then and there, that if there's a Royal Avenue, a Forrest, Tennessee, and a United States of America in heaven, then we're all fucked up.

Walter reached for his gun, dragged himself from the battered vehicle. Up on his feet and in the open air, his head cleared. Over his right shoulder he saw that ten officers had surrounded the white Chevy, smashing out windows, dragging the driver out by his ponytail, delivering malicious kicks to ribs, head, back, and groin, before spreading the suspect face downward and cuffing him. Walter advanced upon the scene, brandishing his gun as if it were a torch welcoming huddled masses to a strange land. "Walt! Walt!" His fellow officers recognized him and grabbed him halfway to where the suspect was being subdued.

"It's over, Walt. We got 'im. Great job! Are you hurt, Walt?" Walter tried to make eye contact with the suspect, who had been scraped from the pavement and tossed into the back of a cruiser. But Ronny McAlister continued to curse and kick at anybody and everything in the world, looking once at Walter as though he didn't exist while the black-and-white sped towards the horizon.

At the station Walter was greeted with pats on the back, smiles and an abundance of oratory accolades that was hung around his head like a laurel. And leading the way was his partner, Joe Hardegree. Walter was immediately summoned to Lieutenant's Peters' office. Suddenly, there was a tremendous throbbing in his ribs.

"Where's your cape and spandex?" Lieutenant Peters pulled off his glasses, chewed the end of one arm. He leaned back in his chair behind his desk, staring at Walter as if he were under a microscope.

"What?"

Lieutenant Peters exploded forward in his seat. "What, my ass! You wanna play Superman from now own you gonna need a cape and a uniform. What in hell were you thinking about, Walt?"

"My fellow officers were in need of assistance—"

"Cut the bullshit. That was stupid, borderline insanity. You could've killed your fellow officers. Innocent people could've been killed. You yourself could've been killed. How do you know that kid didn't have a trunk full of kryptonite?" Lieutenant Peters paused. "No, no. I should've never let your ass come back in this squad room. I should've known you were gonna get involved some way or the other. As of today, you're on mandatory leave of absence. But as of right now I want you to get your ass down to the hospital and get checked out. I think you might have broke your brain." He slipped his glasses back on.

Walter jumped to his feet, startling his supervisor. "Wait a minute, Pete, goddammit! I'm working a case here. I don't need to get checked out, I'm fine. And I don't need no goddam leave of absence. And I sure as hell don't need no fucking shrink the way you're implying. I'm a cop, a detective, and I need to catch a killer, man. Let me do my job."

Lieutenant Peters tried to placate his detective. "You need some time off, Walt. Right now, you're dangerous. You don't give a damn, and a cop that doesn't give a damn doesn't need to be a cop. You're a menace to yourself, this department, and the entire city." He reflected in disbelief. "You're lucky to be alive. A split second later and you would've hit him head on. Nah," he dismissed the whole affair with a wave of his hand, "spend some time with your grandmother, go fishing, think about whether it's really worth being a cop."

"Pete. Listen to me now. I can't just turn around coming down the home stretch. I need to close this case. The city is on the verge of racial chaos. The last three murders in this town are unsolved. I know the bosses are chewing your ass. You need me to close this case. Do me this one favor? Let me close the Williamson case and I'll talk to the shrink, take an LOA or whatever. Just let me make some sense out of things right now."

Lieutenant Peters saw hurt and yearning gather in a pool of tears in the corners of Walter's eye. If the detective had exploded at any point before his very eyes, it would not have surprised him. But it pained Peters to see him this way. He had seen many cops crack and lose it. What was different with Walter Robinson was that he had always seemed to be on the edge and yet under control. That was one of the things that Lieutenant Peters admired: Robinson didn't take things personally. He was competent, professional, and had the makings of a future chief of police written all over him. They could never say that Walter had made it because of affirmative action, like he heard whispered about him from time to time. No. Sometimes he even forgot that Robinson was Black. He never asked for anything, wouldn't accept promotion without merit, demanded only to be afforded the same opportunities as everyone else. And this got him into hot water sometimes with the bosses, who had long memories and short promotional lists. But Lieutenant Peters could always depend on Walter to solve the tough cases and to borrow his ear in matters both professional and personal; he would never confide in his other subordinates. Naturally, before the rest of the squad room, he gnawed on

Robinson's ass, like he did with everyone else. But behind closed doors, he'd come to love him like a father would a son, and it would pain any father to see his son this way. This time, Lieutenant Peters knew, Robinson had slipped, was dangling from the ledge of a precipice. Sure, he could offer advice, even his hand, in relief. But it was ultimately up to Walter to struggle against the situation, overcoming it by the natural ability of his strength or supernatural powers buried deep within.

"Sit down, Walt."

Walter ran his hand through his hair, adjusted the knot of his necktie.

Lieutenant Peters made as though he were busy shuffling papers upon his desk. He pulled his glasses off and tossed them upon the desk, leaning back in his chair. "Did you have a talk with your nephew?"

"Yeah."

"How did it go?"

Walter hunched his shoulders, shook his head. "I don't know. Armageddon seems to be looming on the horizon."

Lieutenant Peters hunched his shoulders. "Why? All three suspects are accounted for now." He reached over to the right side of his desk, grabbed an manila folder, extracted its contents. "We pulled a Jamie Mansfield off a Greyhound bus with a pocketful of jewelry, halfway to Nashville, trying to get to an aunt in Cincinnati. Lee Sumner, the youngest and the dumbest of the three, walked into a pawnshop not once but twice with firearms taken from your grandmother's house. And—"

"All the weapons accounted for?"

"Except one." Lieutenant Peters refocused on the

papers before him. "And you almost killed the last little bastard, Walt. Ronny McAlister." He slid the papers back inside the file, flung it aside, nonchalantly. "Mansfield wrote a two-page confession detailing everything; he wrote so much the goddam pen ran out of ink. Funny, though. I thought the Sumner kid would've cracked first." He sighed heavily. "Now back to your nephew. His demands were that if the suspects were not caught in forty-eight hours there would be hell to pay. We even recovered the weapon used in the attack upon your grandmother, Walt. So what's the problem?"

"The problem is that there is no problem. Nobody has a beef with nobody now. The gangs have called a truce. So even if the suspects are convicted and sentenced, this thing could explode at any moment."

Lieutenant Peters shifted his weight, crossed his legs. "When a dog has to take a leak he finds the nearest tree or fire hydrant and lifts his leg."

Walter returned a blank stare into the smiling face of his boss. "Is this a lesson in Chinese philosophy, Pete?"

"I'm saying," Peters leaned forward on his elbows, "there's been truces and there'll be more truces, but when you gotta go you gotta go. Listen…" he stood, pulled his pants upward while stuffing in his shirt. He walked around his desk, opened the door to his office and barked out Hardegree's name. Then came back to Walter. "We have Cornell Cox in the tomb, Walt." Hardegree poked his head round the door, timorously stepped into the office, and stood beside Walter. "Listen," Lieutenant Peters paced the carpet, his head to the floor, "this guy is guilty as hell. But the problem is that we have very little, if any, evidence to nab this sonofabitch. We don't have evidence or witnesses or nothing. Now, we've held him for an hour already and we can't hold him all night without charging him with something, and if we let him go today without charging him with something we'll never charge him with anything." He stopped in his tracks, narrowed his eyes on his detectives. "Do you guys have any idea what I'm talking about?"

"Yeah, Pete." Detective Hardegree had his hands in his pockets. "Confession."

Walter was on his feet beside his partner, with Lieutenant Peters' smiling face inches from theirs.

"Good. I know you won't let me down."

Detective Hardegree led the way out of the office. Walter followed, his facial expression uneasy. "Is the missing weapon a Remington hunting rifle, Pete?"

"No, Walt," Lieutenant Peters said. "We have that gun. It was the one the kid tried to pawn for drugs," he added as Walter closed the door behind him.

...After I went back into the house to get Ronny we jumped in the old lady's car and got the hell out of there. I was behind the wheel going 90 miles an hour, Ronny was beside me laughing his goddam head off, and Lee was in the back seat whimpering like a little puppy dog. I had to keep telling myself over and over to calm down and not do anything stupid to get us pulled over for speeding or illegal lane change, some bullshit like that. We drove around in circles for what seemed like hours, trying to figure out what to do next. Finally, there's an old building on

Getwell that's been vacant since we were kids and that's where we headed for. It used to be a concrete factory. It's around one in the morning. I circle the building a couple of times to make sure everything is cool and then we get out leaving the car running and the lights on. So, Lee gets the guns out of the back seat, I've got the jewelry and Ronny trails us in to make sure the coast is clear. As soon as he, Ronny, steps foot in the building I blindside him with a right to the chin and knock him on his ass. The gun flies from his waistband and I pick it up and sling it somewhere across the room. Everything is dark, except for the headlights with dust and bugs floating through their beams, and I can hear the gun bouncing across the concrete floor.

What the fuck's wrong with you, man? Ronny shouted, rubbing his jaw and getting to his feet.

I knew he was going to try and hit me back. So before he regained his balance, I grabbed him by the collar and pushed him up against a wall.

I'm gonna beat your ass, I told him.

Lee is standing behind the both of us with his mouth hung open, dropping all the guns on the floor like they were a pile of metal, like he was struck by lightning or something.

Ronny got me off of him with one big push.

You fucked up, Ronny, I screamed at him. You stupid bastard. You fucked us all up.

I didn't fuck nothing up, asshole, he screamed back. I been planning the whole thing from day one. And it went down just the way I wanted. For one time in my life I finally got something right.

Whaddya do, Ronny? Lee stepped forward, his voice materializing from the shadows. You kill that old woman?

What the fuck you think, fatass? Ronny answered past my head, over my right shoulder. I hoped like hell I did. And why the hell you think I did that? 'Cause corpses don't talk. If they do, it's only to other corpses. He was talking to me now. That's the problem with you. I don't expect much from fatass; he don't expect much from himself. But you, he had his finger on the tip of my nose, 'posed to be a fucking genius, but you always think so fucking small. You not as smart as you think you are. All you wanna do is little petty shit and petty shit will get you petty shit every time. Well, I've graduated from that crap. I'm a man. And whatever I have to do I'm willing to do it. Hell, if you're gonna commit a crime, do it so every goddam body will know your name, let 'em remember you for years and years, even after you're dead. I just don't talk a good game, like you, Jamie. I'm through with talking. He hit me in the chest with a two-handed thrust. You better go find my goddam gun, motherfucker, he added.

Ronny and I stood there screaming at each other for about five minutes; I couldn't hear all he was saying and I doubt if he could hear me at all either because our words tangled with each other and then we tangled with each other, wrestling, kicking, biting, while Lee was in the background screaming to himself like he always does whenever he gets upset about anything before he jumped in between us and all three of us were on the floor of the abandoned building that used to be a concrete factory where we used to play as kids. Some kind of way Lee jumped in the middle of us and for a minute it was all legs, arms, fists until he got us apart and we all dusted ourselves off.

Where's my goddam money? Ronny had caught his breath enough to start back screaming at me, but not as loud this time.

I started to go at him again. I never wanted to kill somebody as bad as I wanted to kill him at that moment. But instead I said, what the hell you gonna do now big shot? What's the point in committing a big-time crime if you can't get away with it. Where you running, where you hidin'? You wanna be a big shot but you're just a two-bit, small-time, dumb-ass juvenile delinquent.

Lee was getting ready to say something but Ronny told him if he did he would put his foot down his throat.

I'm just getting started, asshole, Ronny shot back at me. You watch the next couple of days. Just watch and see. I ain't trying to run and hide. If anything, somebody needs to be running and hidin' from me. I'm gonna turn this town inside out. It's gonna take awhile for anybody to catch me and if they do it'll be because I want to be caught.

I reached in my pocket and pulled out the $405 I took from the old lady and divided it three ways.

Ronny snatched the money out of my hand. Ain't nothing around here for me any more. Especially you two. I just buried y'all. For good.

C'mon Ronny, Lee pleaded. We're all friends. Best buddies. Let's make up. You know, we're supposed to be partners for life.

Ronny was backing away, counting his money. Didn't you just hear what I said, fatass? You and Jamie are six feet under and will never be brought back to life as far as I'm concerned. So just put me out of your mind. You'll get over it. Everything has to die sooner or later. He turned and walked into the mouth of night and was swallowed whole. The next thing we heard was the opening and closing of a door, the car burning rubber in a rush to escape.

What are we gonna do now, Jamie? Lee had dropped his money on the ground, was almost in tears, running but his feet not taking him anywhere.

Lee, listen to me, I said, grabbing him and shaking him by the shoulders.

How are we going to get home, Jamie? He was almost in tears.

Fuck that, man! I tried to calm him down.

But it's so dark out here, Jamie. He was running but his feet were taking him nowhere.

Lee, I slapped him hard across the face, listen to me, goddammit, and listen good. He looked at me as though he'd just woke up from a coma. You need to find a place to lay low for awhile, a long while. They're coming after us. And they're coming hard. But that's OK. You know who cased the house, right? You know who raped and killed the old woman, right? You know who's in her car right now, right?

I'm scared, Jamie.

I know. But it's alright, man. Let's go home.

I hid the guns underneath a pile of bricks and other shit over in a corner the best I could. Then I stumbled back to where we were standing and picked up up the money Lee had dropped and stuffed it back into my pockets. Lee just stood there staring into the darkness as if he could see something I couldn't see. After that we walked home trying to avoid passing cars, well-lit streets and the eye contact of friends and strangers.

Signed, Jamie Mansfield

Detectives Robinson and Hardegree removed their weapons before entering "the tomb." It was eight-by-twelve feet of concrete, confinement and constraint, save for a bay window shielded by blinds providing an open eye to the squad room, opposite which was a bulletin board covered with a plain white sheet. On an adjacent wall, spanning its width, was a two-way mirror behind which lay a closet-sized room where a machine recorded the tête-à-tête of suspect and detective to tape recorders and timelessness. The walls were covered with several coats of drabness.

Walter entered the room first, Detective Hardegree closing the door behind him. They stood shoulder to shoulder, looking at the suspect, who sat slumped in his chair behind a wooden table, leering.

Walter walked over to the suspect, stood over him with his face implacable as stone.

"What?" The suspect turned his nose up at Walter as if he were a bad odor.

Walter grabbed the table and tossed it into the corner of the room, its impact as it landed dislodging one leg. The suspect jumped to his feet screaming what the fuck and goddam and crazy motherfuckers.

"Sit down!" Walter stood close enough to smell the suspect's breath and tell what he had for dinner the day before yesterday. The suspect, confused and angry, strengthened his resolve. "Sit down!"

"Hey, Cornell." Detective Hardegree wedged himself between his partner and the suspect. "This is Detective Robinson. Detective Robinson, this is Cornell Cox." He patted Cox on the shoulder. "It's alright, man. Have a seat."

Walter pulled up two chairs and he and Detective Hardegree sat directly across from Cox, their knees almost touching, their physical presence pressing down upon him like the falling sky.

"Why'd you do it, Cornell?" Walter.

"Do what?"

"Can I get you something to drink, Cornell?" Detective Hardegree.

"I don't have time for any bullshit. Telissa. Why'd you kill her?"

"Man, I don't know what you talkin' 'bout."

"What about a cigarette? You smoke, Cornell?"

"You know exactly what I'm talking about."

"You got the wrong man, Officer."

"Where'd you hide the knife, Cornell?"

"Turkey and ham. You hungry, Cornell?"

"I don't know nothing 'bout no knife."

"How did you lure her way out in the country like that?"

"Look, man. I don't want nothing to eat, nothing to drink, or no cigarettes. I just wanna go home, and I'm telling y'all for the last time I didn't kill nobody."

Walter slowly erupted into volcanic laughter, hollow, sardonic, spewing reverberations, spreading like red-hot lava from wall to wall. Abruptly, he cut it off as if mirth flowed through hot and cold spigots. "You can't even say her name, you little bastard. Say it."

"Whose name?"

"Say her name." Walter reached over and grabbed Cox.

"Walt, Walt." Detective Hardegree was on his feet, trying to intervene.

"Get off me, man. I ain't saying nothing."

"Te-lee-sa. Say it, motherfucker."

All three men were on their feet, engaged in a tango of pleads and curses, until Detective Hardegree dislodged his partner's hands from around the neck of the suspect. He grabbed Walter and marched him towards the door.

"Relax, Walt, relax." He looked over his shoulder and lowered his voice. "Let me take a shot at him. Get some air or something. He ain't going nowhere." He patted Walter on the shoulder, opened the door for him.

"I'm sorry, Cornell," Detective Hardegree said closing the door after Walter and retaking his seat, "my partner is a little intense. You sure I can't get you anything?"

"Yeah. Why don't you get another partner?"

Sitting at his desk with his head in his hands, Walter noticed the pain in his side increasing in intensity. Maybe it had been there since the wreck and he had only just now become cognizant of it or maybe it had been there all of his life. Anyway, it hurt like hell. He reached into his desk drawer, emancipated a couple of aspirin from a plastic bottle and popped them in his mouth. He removed Telissa's diary from the drawer before throwing the bottle of painkillers inside, sliding it shut and lighting a cigarette. He flipped its pages, reading occasional sentences through rings of exhaled smoke.

08/16:

It is a blessing to be alive and to have seen another day. I feel there is nothing I can't do, nothing I can't be and nowhere that I cannot go. And if anything were to happen to me right this minute, I couldn't complain but would have to thank God for it all. I just want to be the best teacher that I can possibly be in the time that I'm allotted on this earth. There is nothing more joyous than to see a child's face glow from the light of understanding. I love teaching fourth grade. That is what my gift is and that is what I want to do. Now, diary, if I could be so disciplined in my choice of men it would indeed be a perfect world. But it's no use playing games, I'm getting too old for that. I still have feelings for Lucas. Always did. He may not be a professional in a three-piece suit, but he is a good man. Hard working, drug free and knows who he is. OK, I love him. There, I said it. That's one reason why I haven't returned Cornell's phone calls for the last three days, not to mention that damn rap music. He's still 17 years old, mentally. He cares more about how shiny the rims are on his car, the latest sneakers and the newest CD (and I don't mean certificate of deposit) than he does about his future. I guess that's what I get for dating a guy four years younger than me. I mean, whenever we're together, he has to blast that damn rap music and I can't stand it. He doesn't know what he wants out of life whereas Lucas is comfortable where he is and doesn't want to budge. That's one of the things I love about Lucas, stubbornness. But who am I to talk, I haven't been perfect. And the older I get the more I learn that if your heart is not into something it's no use faking it and it's no use seeing Cornell again. And before long, I'll have to tell Lucas how I really feel. Who says I can't have a career, husband, and kids? Lord have mercy on me and my decision about choosing men. But I know that no matter what, you are always with me. Goodnight.

Walter extinguished the cigarette and flipped through the remaining pages of the daily chronicle of the life of Telissa Williamson. He slammed the book shut, frustrated at his inability to detect evidence among its paragraphs or a smoking gun concerning her killer hidden between pages.

All he had was her frustration at failed relationships—something he really didn't want to hear about right now—and a baseball cap recovered at the scene of the crime. He slid another cigarette from the pack and was in the process of lighting it when Detective Rawls's laughter glided across his ear from an adjacent desk. Walter watched Detective Rawls on the phone, inquiring about his son and delighting in the relayed exploits of the four-year-old. Robinson blew out the match without lighting the cigarette. Where was Sherry? What was she doing? What was she and his—their—baby, doing? Hell, he didn't have any doubts about it being his kid. Yes. He was responsible for creating a new life. Father. The word frightened him to the edge of panic. What in hell did he know about being a father? Why weren't there any academies where fathers-to-be could take a six-week training course and graduate with a certificate of completion? Sure, there were manuals at the local bookstore to provide didactic instruction. But what you learned in a book didn't have a damned thing to do with real life. He'd learned that a long time ago; it was all on-the-job training. He knew he had to clothe, feed, and shelter. Those were duties and were no problem. It was the responsibility of bringing a new life into the world, holding it in his arms, changing its diapers and having it totally dependent on him, Walter Lewis Robinson, that gave him the most trepidation. From now on his life and actions would be a paragon for his newborn flesh. He had the responsibility of nurturing, teaching, and disciplining in a world that would try to demolish everything he instilled in his child once it set foot beyond the threshold of home. And even if he expelled his final breath and spent his last atom of energy in being the ultimate father, it was no guarantee. The flesh of his flesh would not be his for ever. His offspring would have to find his or her own beauty, love, dreams, understanding, peace, God, tomorrows, forged by his or her own hands. And that could lead either to triumph or tragedy, probably both, on the road paved with the shadow of light. Walter Robinson knew how indifferent this world could be. He had never wanted a child of his to live in such a world. But there was nothing he could do about it now. Sherry was gone, and maybe for good. But he would resolve to always be in the life of his child, unlike his father before him. Not be perfect, not always right, not always wrong. Just be. No Black boy should have to go through this world without a father.

Walter had been staring into nothingness, and when his ruminations lost their luster, Sergeant Riggs was staring back at him, daggers gazing from his eyes. Walter rose from his chair and meandered toward the tomb, measuring the sergeant with deliberate intent, pausing before entering the room, giving him a final once-over as if he were a virulent antibody to be avoided and abhorred.

Inside, he found his partner engaged with the suspect in discussing Labron James versus Kobe Bryant, Fords as opposed to Chevies, like old buddies catching up on old times. Cox was sipping a soft drink, his upper lip stained with orange soda. Walter closed the blinds on the room's only window, turned his chair around, and straddled it.

"Where were you Saturday night, Cornell?" Walter's voice was low and even.

Cornell Cox was light complected, bore the scars from a bad case of teenage acne, had high cheekbones, hair twisted into miniature dreadlocks and by slouching sideways in his seat made his five-foot-eight frame seem smaller than it was. As soon as Walter had re-entered the room he erected a wall of attitude and aloofness.

"Over my girlfriend's house."

"What's her name and address?"

He smacked his lips, smirked. "Sheila Hunt. 43 Westwood Drive."

"You're lying, Cornell!" Detective Hardegree leaned forward, shouted into the suspect's face, his voice and personality changing faster than the snap of a finger. "And when people lie to us, that insults our intelligence. Have I insulted your intelligence, Cornell? Have I? No, of course not. I've treated you with all the dignity and respect I know how, and I expect you to give the same back to me. Now, when you say you were at your girlfriend's house you're disrespecting me 'cause, number one, I talked to Sheila Hunt of 43 Westwood and she hasn't seen you in weeks, let alone a couple of nights ago, and she also said that she was your ex-girlfriend, and see, that's what I mean by insulting my intelligence, because when you tell me some shit like that what you're really saying is this dumb sonofabitch, meaning me, don't know how to do his homework before he takes a test. I've done my homework on Sheila, your family, on Telissa, on you. And let me tell you, man, if I had to take a test on you, I'd ace that sonofabitch in a heartbeat. You know why? Because all I'd have to do is answer every question with the word: loser. Either loser or two-time loser. But you know in spite of all of that, I've tried to be nice to you. Have I not been nice to you? Where were you Saturday night, Cornell?"

Cornell looked at Detective Hardegree like he wanted to rub his eyes to make sure he was looking at the same person as five minutes ago. "I ain't asked you to be nice to me. I ain't asked nobody for a goddam thang. I told you where I was. How you know *she* ain't lying?"

"She ain't got no reason to lie," Detective Hardegree rebutted.

"How you know? She ever been your girlfriend?"

"I don't know, Joe," interrupted Walter, "I think she was lying too."

Detective Hardegree, exasperated, placed one hand on his knee and the other over his mouth and looked at his partner as if he wanted to slap the excrement out of him.

"You ever been in love, Cornell?" Walter didn't give him time to respond in the affirmative or the negative. "I'm not talking about no Sheila Hunt or some other skank. I'm talking about a reeeaaal woman. Like Telissa Williamson. Huh? Yeah, you know what I'm talkin' 'bout. Yeah, you been in love before and it wasn't a pleasant experience either, huh? I understand, I been there."

"Man, I don't know where you've been and I really don't care. Y'all wasting my time. I gotta go to work."

"Work can wait," jabbed Detective Hardegree, "wait like it always does. You can't hold a job longer than two months at a time anyway." He arched his eyebrows. "Homework."

Walter continued as if he were in the room all alone, engrossed in an auditory daydream. "Yeah, Telissa. You was in love the first time y'all met. Here you are just minding your own business on a Wednesday afternoon, doing your job in the maintenance department at the general hospital and you meet this little tasty piece coming to visit a sick coworker, and she actually took the time to talk to you! And took your phone number and called you too! I mean, man, here's this slim brown, with a master's degree, nice ride, sharp crib, a bank, and she diggin' you. Sheeeeit, fuck Sheila Hunt! You a straight-up player if there ever was one and I know you tapped that ass like it never been tapped. But being in love, Cornell, and I found this out and you know it now, is sweet and all but it also has thorns that cut like a mother. I mean, deep down inside you know you're just a hood rat drifting from day to day with no goals no ambition, just hoping something good is going to happen to you instead of going out and making something good happen; I ain't mad atcha, man. You sitting at the table and the game being played is poker but Telissa was playing blackjack. And Telissa, that's such a pretty name, she finally realizes who you are too. Maybe she was trying to forget a former lover or maybe she was just horny but that got old and she didn't want you to be in love with her any more, but you had fallen in too deep and the fall was long and sweet. You begged, pleaded, promised, and when that didn't work you thought maybe slapping her around a bit would do it. But you found out that Telissa didn't mind getting slapped as long as she could slap back." Walter, with a wan smile spreading across his face, dropped his gaze from the ceiling right into the eyes of Cornell. "You loved that girl, boy. You didn't mean to kill her, didn't want to kill her. But you didn't want to lose her and things got out of control. It's OK, Cornell. Passion is a sonofabitch. You're not its first victim and until the world ends you won't be its last." His smile stretched across his face. "Am I right? You know I am. C'mon, help yourself out."

A vein had creased the forehead of Cornell, angry and throbbing. "So what? When did love and passion get to be a crime? I'm tired of these bullshit games, man."

"It ain't no crime." Walter shook his head. "And you know what? Like I said, I believe you. I don't think you meant to kill her. You could've shot that girl. You could've beat that girl with a baseball bat or a tire iron. But you stabbed that girl, Cornell. You can't get no more intimate than that. Every time you plunged that blade into her that was like making love to her for the final time. It was death, but it was death in the name of love that's the crime, man."

"Look," Cornell sat on the edge of his chair, pointing his finger from one detective to the other, "I've been in enough of these rooms to know my rights. Either cut me loose or I want a lawyer. Y'all ain't got nothin'."

"I'll tell you what we got, asshole." Detective Hardegree sprang to his feet, overturning his chair and ripped the white sheet of paper from the bulletin board. "We got the woman you love and she is calling your name and pointing her finger at you and she wants you to tell her fourth-grade class that she won't be in tomorrow morning or any other morning." Thumbtacked to the bulletin board were autopsy photos of the naked body of Telissa Williamson in various poses with closeups of numerous stab wounds to her torso. Cornell looked to his left, his face in a paroxysm of horror. Just as quickly he donned a mask of equanimity as he turned back.

"Cornell," Detective Hardegree faced the suspect, his index finger on a photo behind him, "look at the board, Cornell! This is your last chance to tell Telissa how much you really love her." He snatched a photo from the board, marched over to Cornell and stuffed it under his nose. "Telissa, this is Cornell. Cornell say hello to Telissa. Say her name, motherfucker. What's her name?" Detective Hardegree held the photo in one hand and the back of Cornell's head in the other. "Say her name. Where's the knife, Cornell?"

Cornell freed himself from the grip of Detective Hardegree and pushed him halfway across the room, spilling his orange soda over him and the floor. "Get up off me, honky motherfucker. Both of y'all just back the fuck up. Back up and let me out of this room right now. Y'all ain't got jack on me. I see the whole thing. You ain't got witnesses, no weapon, no nothing. Who the hell y'all think y'all messing with? I told y'all I didn't do nothing, nothing to nobody. So either charge me with something or get me a lawyer. Either way just stop fucking with me." His breathing was rapid, his hands balled into fists. "Y'all don't know me." His eyes flashed from one detective to the other, his finger pointing squarely at the nose of Walter. "But I know you. You're the detective that solved my sister's rape five years ago. Remember me?"

"I know your family, son," Walter nodded.

"Yeah, my family thought that dude was gonna walk and he was about to too, until you busted him with that DNA shit—I don't even know what the hell DNA stands for—but there wasn't a damn thing he could say or do about who he was and how much of himself he left behind after breaking into my sister's apartment. That much I know. Yeah, you got a rep on the street. I know you. But you don't know a damn thing about me. Just because you got my rap sheet, so what? How many niggers *ain't* been to jail before? Think I ain't never been in love before? Think I ain't never had no rich pussy before? White girls, Black girls, Hispanics, Orientals, hell, it don't make no difference. I'm the daddy of the Mack Daddy. I always keep more than one woman and when I get tired of one, I love 'em and leave 'em. I'm a heartbreaker man, a natural-born player. I ain't trippin' over no chick, dead or alive. You want me to look at some pictures, I'll look at 'em. You want me to say her name? Alright. But it ain't gonna change nothing and it ain't gonna make no difference about nothing and when I get through with those pictures and saying her name as many times as you want, get me a lawyer, 'cause I ain't taking no mo' shit from either of y'all." He eased himself back into his seat, folded his arms across his chest and crossed his legs, like a potentate after promulgating edicts to the proletariat.

Detective Hardegree looked at his partner, shrugged his shoulders.

"Alright, man. I'll get you a lawyer." Walter arched his eyebrows and exited the room.

Detective Hardegree stood over Cornell. He shook his head for several minutes before speaking and pacing the floor. "That ain't gonna do no good Cornell. That's only gonna make it worse. We're gonna get you a lawyer. And you know what kind of lawyer. Court-appointed lawyer. Court-appointed lawyer that's got a case-load of clients up to his ass. Court-appointed lawyer that's half prepared. Court-appointed lawyer you've dealt with before." He stopped pacing the floor, stood in front of Cornell. "You'd be better off talking to us. That court-appointed lawyer is gonna get you lethal injection, Cornell. Just tell us the truth and we can work something out, man."

"I'll take my chances with the court-appointed lawyer. All of 'em ain't bad. Just like all cops ain't bad." He began to pick dirt from beneath his fingernails. "I ain't got nothing else to say to you."

Detective Hardegree picked up the table from the corner, set it upright in front of Cornell, and wondered how he would ever get those orange stains out of his pants. With the photo still in his hand, he began to remove the others from the bulletin board. He wanted to apologize to Telissa, as he'd done to other victims of murder whose killers hadn't been brought to justice. He heard the door open like a thunderclap and turned to see a blue baseball cap floating through the air.

"Cornell!"

Walter stood in the doorway, his arm still suspended in the throwing motion, the cap landing on the table before Cornell like a ripe melon on a concrete floor.

"You almost pulled it off, Cornell," Walter said, leaning against the doorjamb, legal pad and pen in hand. "You almost got away with murder, dogg. All you had to do was go back and get your cap. Your cap! The same cap with your hair inside. The cap, Cornell, with your DNA, deoxyribonucleic acid, all over it. Of all the people in the world there's only one Cornell Cox and your genetic blueprint—yeah, that's a good word for it—is on the inside of that cap. We ain't got no knife, no witness, no alibi. But we got this baseball cap and that's the same as having you."

Cornell fingered the baseball cap front and back, rotated it on his index finger like a helicopter rotor, studied it as though it were a ghost of skin, bone and flesh come to haunt all the twenty-five years of his life. He gently laid the cap upon the table, straightened it like a sacred object to be revered; then put his head in his hands. Detective Hardegree had to do everything in his power to stop himself from jumping up and down; instead he smiled and continued removing photos from the wall.

Walter closed the door behind him, turned his seat around, pushed the pad and pen inches from Cornell's lowered head. "It's over, Cornell," he sighed, talking to the top of Cornell's head. "No more lies to cover the other lies. No more seeing Telissa's face every time you go to sleep. No more having trouble keeping food down. No more worrying about when we gonna pick you up and bring you down here. You can breathe now. You're free. I know you didn't mean to kill that girl and I'll make sure everybody else knows it too."

Cornell raised his head just as Detective Hardegree was sitting down. Walter slid the pen and paper in front of the suspect. "Help yourself out, son."

Cornell wiped his mouth with the back of his hand, nervously tugged at the braids in his hair, hesitated. "I just wanted to scare her. I would've did whatever she asked me to do. But she said there wasn't nothing I could or couldn't do. And then she tried to scare me from scaring her and that wasn't a good idea. I just wanted to be with her for the rest of my life, that's all I cared about."

He picked up the pen, paused to organize the words in his head, and began to compose a confession of murder.

Later in the afternoon, after Detective Hardegree had booked the suspect into the criminal justice system, typed a final report, erased Telissa Williamson's red-inked name and rewritten it in black on the homicide board, he found

Walter taking a smoke in a designated area adjacent to the precinct. The area was a brick patio, trimmed with shrubbery, adorned with picnic tables, and shaded by a canopy of shadows. Walter was standing at the edge of the patio, imbibing the panorama of the city.

"Hey, partner," Detective Hardegree announced upon approach.

Walter answered without turning around. "Hey, Joe. Where you going with that gun in your hand?"

"Haha. That's one of my favorite songs. How'd you know I like Jimi?"

"Everybody likes Jimi."

They stood shoulder to shoulder, Detective Hardegree loosening his tie, removing his jacket, and folding it over his forearm. He slurped from a can of diet soda. "When did the lab results on that cap come back?"

"I don't know."

"How did you know the cap tested positive for Cornell's DNA?"

Walter expelled a stream of smoke. "I didn't."

Detective Hardegree choked on his beverage, turned his coughs into an outburst of laughter. "Goddam, Walt. You're the best man! I thought for sure we'd lost that bastard. You think he didn't really mean to kill her?" He took another swallow to soothe his irritated throat.

"At this point, I really don't care."

"You think the confession will hold in court? After all, he did ask for a lawyer."

"I know what he asked for. And I was going to get him a lawyer. I just gave the man his cap and he started talking. All I know is we got a confession. The bosses are happy.

Pete is happy and I guess we're supposed to be happy. I guess when we tell Telissa's mom and her baby sister that we got a confession, they'll be happy too. But you know what?" He dropped his cigarette, extinguished it with the bottom of his shoe. "I look out over this city and I find it hard to find happiness. If anything people are angry at happiness. They're either angry at it or unhappy about it. And whether you're a victim or a victimizer, it all comes full circle sooner or later. And the hell of it is, I have no answers, only questions: how long and what's the point?"

"Why do we suffer? That's what you're asking, Walt? Why does man suffer?"

"We've seen a helluva lot of things out here on these streets, Joe. Babies sodomized, homeless people set afire, old women butchered." Images of his grandmother flashed across his mind in successive frames.

"Well," Hardegree finished his soda, tossing the can into a refuse container, "yeah, you're right. And we'll probably see a helluva lot worse the way things are going. But let me ask you something, Walt: why does God suffer?"

"God suffers?" He looked at his partner for the first time.

"I would think so. If I had to deal with a contrary sonofabitch like you, I'd suffer too."

Walter nodded his head, stifled a laugh. "I'm serious, Joe. We've been told that God is good, God is love, that God so loved the world that He gave His only begotten Son…well, all of that just don't make any sense when I look at all of that." He pointed his index finger like an indictment against the outstretched city. "Since you're an authority on God, when did God stop caring?"

"Nah," Detective Hardegree shook his head, "I'm not an authority on God or anything else. But I do know that God hasn't stop caring. Or loving. Yeah, there's a lot of bad things going on in this world, but just think if God had stopped caring, this world would have self-destructed a long time ago. That much I know. God still cares, God still loves, and God still saves."

"Why didn't he save Tellissa Williamson?"

"How do you know He didn't? From what I read in her diary, sounds like He saved her along time ago. See Walt, you're getting God and man mixed up. What you see out here," he included the city skyline with a sweep of his arm, "is man at his best and man at his best is about as depraved as you can get. This world has fallen and it can't get up, not by itself anyway. All the rape, robbery, murder, that's man, and when I say man that's both male and female man, the human race that has chosen to reject Him."

"Him? How do you know God is a Him? What if He is a Her?"

"I don't and it wouldn't matter. I'll apologize when I see Her."

"OK, but tell me this. I understand that God gives us free will to either choose or reject Him—for the sake of argument, we'll say Him. But if you don't choose Him, you're banished to hell for eternity, right? What kind of free will is that?"

"That's all the free will we need. Yeah, Walt, we're free to choose or not to choose, but hell, we don't control the consequences. We know the consequences, but we don't control them. If we controlled them, then we'd be God."

The sun was sinking beyond the horizon as if the

ground had pulled a stopper, allowing it to gurgle into the earth. A slight breeze and a glow of iridescence wafted across the patio.

Walter turned, faced his partner. "So you're saying all we should worry about is getting to heaven, wherever that is, and in the meantime be oblivious to all the pain and suffering and the people who're made in the image of God who're doing the paining and suffering? Is that what choosing God is all about?"

"Walt, I haven't said any of that. But if you want to say it, fine. I'm saying this: when you choose God, really choose Him, Heaven is on the inside of you and someone will see God in you and the works you do and if the world needs anything it needs to see God in the office or on the playing field or at home."

"Sometimes I wonder even about that. You got some sincere people trying to live their faith—hell, I believe you're one of 'em, Joe. But while you out here trying to do right, walk right and be right, you might as well be spitting into the wind, man. I mean, we've seen some bastards do some mean things and some of 'em got what they deserved, but most of 'em are driving Lexuses and wearing Rolexes with houses in the hills some goddam where, living to be decrepit old bastards. So hell, why should I beat myself up trying to do something halfway right when doing something all the way wrong comes out on top?"

Detective Hardegree shifted his jacket from one arm to the other. "I wouldn't worry about it too much, Walt. Things are out of joint right now. But Jesus Christ is real and he is coming back—"

"Man, Jesus Christ got be a goddam fool to come back

down here, or come back from wherever he is. What the hell for? They done run him off once. This time they gonna give him the electric chair. I heard He liked to fish. If I was Him, I'd get me a yacht and call the whole thing off." He spat on the ground. "I know from Sunday School after God made the world the first time He sat back and said, 'That's good.' I wonder what the hell He would say now?"

Detective Hardegree's laughter tumbled out past the patio's edge. "That's funny. But Jesus'll be in an ass-kicking mode when He comes back this time, Walt. He won't be negotiating and pleading and turning either cheek. The score'll be even: wheat, chaff, goats, sheep, the abandoned, the embraced. Yeah," he looked wistfully into the sky, "I wouldn't worry about it too much, those bastards that are getting away with murder and a little bit of everything on the side, real judgment is coming."

"Let me ask you something, preacher." Walter stuck a cigarette in his mouth, fumbled in his pockets for a book of matches, "If God created the world, is in control of it, has done what He wanted to do with it, what in hell difference does it make how I live my life when His will is going to be done regardless?"

"Because you love the truth, Walt. You've been loving it all your life. And loving the truth means you're not afraid to follow wherever it leads, and like any journey, the first step starts in the mirror. When I said you were the best, that's what I meant. Right now, I know you're seeing through a glass darkly—that's Paul—we all are." Walter thought about the scene in Witherspoon's kitchen. "But the light is not far away, one day all will be revealed. But just stay the course. You're closer to God than you think."

Walter lit his cigarette, blew out the match. "Now that's some scary shit. But I tell you what I think. Sometimes I think God up in heaven looking down at us and He's laughing His ass off saying, 'You stupid motherfuckers. Why don't y'all leave me the hell alone and get up off your lazy asses and do something for yourselves and stop being so afraid of life.'" He released a gush of laughter, acrid with smoke and sarcasm. "And I'm about to bring a kid into all this."

"Kid?" Detective Hardegree's glee was uncontainable. "Sherry's pregnant and you didn't even tell your partner?"

"Don't feel left out. I just found out this morning."

"Congratulations, Walt!" Detective Hardegree put arm his around his shoulder, gave him a hug. "You old rascal, you. Who would've thunk it! How do you feel?"

"Right now, the only thing I feel is this pain in my ribs which you sure as hell ain't helping." He tried to push Hardegree away from him. "I never wanted kids, you know that. But the more I think about it, I guess I could get used to it."

"Man," Hardegree released his grip, "let me tell you something. Having children is the best thing that ever happened to me. When I go home at the end of the day and hear the word 'daddy' before Michael and Hannah jump into my arms, I feel like they are equalizers against all the stuff we've being talking about that goes on these streets. From watching 'em come into this world to seeing them take their first steps to crying when they cry and laughing when they laugh, it's all a miracle to me. That's the beauty of children." He shifted his weight from one foot to the other. "Like Michael, he's six, right? So the other night I put him to bed and he asks, 'Dad, can I have some chocolate milk?' I say no, it's bedtime. Lights out. About five minutes later, he hollers out, 'Daaaddd?' I say what. He says again, 'Can I have some chocolate milk?' I tell him he's not getting anything to drink this late at night and if he asks again I'm going to come in there and spank him. So about five more minutes later, he hollers again and, check this out, Walt, he says 'Dad, when you come in here to spank me can you bring some chocolate milk with ya,'" Detective Hardegree doubled over with laughter. "Kids are something else, man. They either drive you crazy or maintain your sanity." A pleasant thought skipped across his face. "Man, I can see you now. Daddy Walt. How's Mama Sherry?"

"Gone."

"Gone where?"

"Gone." Walter's eye contact underscored his words. "Gone as in split. Gone as in goodbye. Gone as in can't take any more of me."

Detective Hardegree's smile faded like the moon in the morning. "What does all that mean, Walt?"

"I tell you what it means. It means that I'm going to take some time off. For how long? Might be a month, might be for ever. I don't know how much more I can give or how much more I can give away." He slung his cigarette on the ground. "I know one thing. Ever since Sherry said she was pregnant, feels like I'm living somebody's else life."

They turned, began walking back toward the squad room. "Yeah, your life is about to change now." Hardegree changed the subject quickly. "So, you're gonna see the shrink, huh?"

"Why is nothing a goddam secret around here unless

everybody knows about it?" They walked on in silence before entering a precinct side door. "Looks like I gained a child and lost a wife, Joe. Is that the way it normally works?"

Detective Hardegree slipped on his jacket. "Do you want her to be lost, Walt? Then do something about it. Anyway, as long as I've been knowing you, you've never done anything the normal way."

Walter yanked the door, grimaced from the pain of the exertion. "I think I cracked some ribs. I better get checked out."

"Alright, Walt. If you need anything, let me know. Hey," again he changed the subject as if he were switching channels on a TV, "what's the latest on that fax, man?"

"Still up in the air. I don't feel good about it."

"Yeah, well…had the strangest feeling somebody was trailing me today." Hardegree nodded his head slowly.

Walter furrowed his brow in concern. Thought of his nephew but dismissed the idea; forty-eight hours wasn't up yet. "You sure? Get a look at 'em?"

"Nah," Hardegree shook his head this time, "I tried to give chase but lost them." He switched the conversation back to its original station. "Any idea how long you'll be off, Walt?" They were standing at their work areas now.

Walter was removing personal items from his desk drawer. "I really don't, Joe. My grandmother is gonna need somebody to look after her for awhile. I think some time in the peace and quiet of the country would do me some good. Whatcha think?"

"Yeah…I mean…" The telephone on Detective Hardegree's desk rang as if someone shouted "fire" in a packed discotech with one way in and one way out. Walter had collected his belongings, patted his partner goodbye on the shoulder.

"Homicide, Hardegree. Yeah. Where at? Hold on a minute." He looked up from note-taking, secured the phone between ear and shoulder, and covered the mouthpiece with his hand. "Hey, Walt. Wait up a minute, willya?"

Walter walked out of the squad room without looking back.

On his way out of the precinct doors, Walter Robinson began to shed his jacket and tie as if they were a bad habit. Before entering his Chrysler, he tossed them onto the back seat, stood with his back against the driver's door, and looked into the sky. He felt a sharp pain in the back of his left shoulder and without turning around knew it was a piece of plastic molding that had come loose from the window frame. Ah, his car, his Chrysler. It was like a well-worn pair of socks or your favorite chair. He knew what was on it, what was in it and who put it there. Walter doubted if he'd ever get rid of the damn thing. Like some guys on the force, he could've driven the department-issued vehicles home. But there is nothing as uncool as driving an unmarked cop car twenty-four hours a day. Besides, he'd just wrecked the hell out of that anyway.

The world above moved with a briskness of cloud and shadow forewarning of rain and relief. He remembered the last time the sky looked this way. It was his sixteenth summer and Mrs Mabel Scott's baby got killed and that big oak crashed through Big Mama's house. It was supper time, around six in the evening, and there was fresh corn, okra, sliced tomatoes, pot roast, lemonade, cornbread on the table and the news breaking in on John Wayne shooting Indians warning everybody in the county and the surrounding vicinity to take cover immediately. The old folks had seen many a storm before, saw the signs of their coming and knew this was gonna be a big one, even though the big ones usually happened in the spring. But Walter heard only the stillness of country air and then sheets of hail fashioned into baseballs that peppered his body, their bodies, as Big Mama dragged him by the hand, running for the root cellar, running through midnight at six in the evening with the sky rent into halves by a dagger of lightning, the thunder rumbling the way your stomach does when you haven't eaten in a while and you don't want anyone else to know it, and the wind that materialized as out of a nightmare like the bogeyman hoboing a freight train, taking over its controls, before he and Big Mama, the earth about to swallow them in one gulp, wrenched open the cellar door and tumbled downward into cobwebs and darkness, Big Mama gathering him to her bosom and urging him to "Pray, boy, pray." But Walter could only look up and wonder about the sounds surrounding him, the cows that seemed to have sprouted wings and taken flight, trees bearing pickup trucks, the hinges of the root cellar door rattling threnodies, human screams fading in and out like static on distant radio stations, and Big Mama imploring, "Pray, boy, pray."

Minutes later, they emerged from underground into the coolness of air, sunshine, birdsong and the earth thrashed by Mother Nature's temper tantrum. And then when Grandaddy showed up from town Big Mama started crying and saying thank you, Jesus, and they hugged each other and talked about the tree through the roof and somebody discovered Mrs Scott's baby girl about a half-mile away beneath mud and trees and the family hound Blue emerged at Walter's heel, while he stood there with his hands in his pockets in the shadow of Grandaddy and Big Mama still hugging each other and now Grandaddy was crying too.

Walter slid behind the wheel of the automobile and recalled that Mrs Mabel Scott had two other children after that summer of '75. He grimaced. No matter if he moved the wrong way or moved too quickly, his ribs hurt. Driving along, he looked at the sky once again. With the windows down, the air smelled of rain. He grabbed his cell phone and, keeping his eyes on the road, hit speed dial. Marcia's phone rang three times, activating the answering machine. Marcia Slack had been Sherry's new best friend for the past five years. He knew his wife was holed up not receiving phone calls, visits or the Pony Express. When troubled she preferred bubble baths and cold glasses of white wine.

"Sherry? Sherry. Pick up, baby."

He importuned a second and third time. "I'm not hanging up this phone until I talk to you."

Marcia picked up. "Walter. How are you doing? She can't come to the phone right now. Can I take a message, please?"

"Marcia...yeah, you can take this message for me. Put my wife on the phone right now. I don't have time to play. How come you ain't out on a date?"

Marcia popped masticated food in his ear and he could see her with her head cocked at an angle, pouring a glass of grapefruit juice, impatiently tapping one foot against the floor. "She doesn't want to talk to you or anybody right now, Walter. And my love life is none of your business. And just for that remark I think I'll hang up. Don't you have some innocent people to frame or somebody to beat down or something? Goodbye."

"Marcia, if you hang up on me, I'll be banging on your door in about two minutes. You said she doesn't want to talk to me? Put her on the phone and let me hear her say she doesn't want to talk to me. Otherwise, you're gonna have to call the police to get me off your porch."

Marcia Slack was a broker for a investment firm. "That suits me just fine. Some of the biggest criminals are cops anyway. Somebody should've called the police on the police a long time ago. But it wouldn't have done any good. They would've covered it up like they always do."

Walter turned from Walker Road into McDaniel Drive. "Well, hell, don't bother to call the police any more next time you hear a noise outside your house at three in the morning. Look, I ain't trying to argue with you and I know why you ain't got no man. But don't take it out on me, OK? Let me tell you something, the sooner you come out of the closet and stop repressing those emotions, the sooner you won't be so hostile." He went from tones of confidentiality to almost shouting. "Now, put my wife on this goddam phone."

"I can't argue with that. You're such a brilliant man. Maybe that's why, after your wife stays here awhile, she might not ever want leave. Goodbye, Walter."

Walter anticipated the abruptness of sudden silence

following the termination of the phone call. Instead, he heard the whisper of muffled voices and a rustle of movement.

"Walter Lewis Robinson. Why are you disrespecting my friends?" Sherry had negotiated the receiver from Marcia, who could still be heard fuming in the background, fading into the distance.

"Friends? Baby, you need to get the hell out of there. You can do better than that. How you doing? I called to talk to you anyway."

"I don't know. I should be asking you that. Did you see that car you were driving?"

"See it? Hell, I was in it, remember?" His laughter thundered into her ear.

"You could've killed your fool self trying to play Supernigger."

"Thanks for showing so much concern. Why did I have to call you first?"

She stammered, hesitated. "I don't know. I started to call but...I don't know. The main thing is that you're alright."

Walter came to a four-way stop, turned right on Prince Edward. "I'm still breathing, but I don't know if I'm alive."

Sherry didn't reply, as if pondering the purpose of his words. "Meaning?"

"Meaning that there is no living without you, Sherry. To go on living without you would be like going from day to day without both legs or arms or eyes. I couldn't function like that."

"You would adjust. People do it all the time. There are wheelchairs, prosthetics. Blind people lead productive lives."

"Hey, cut that out. But what would I do without a heart? And no other heart will do. You've always seen the best of what I could have become, encouraging me to do better and never criticizing my failures, most of which I was to blame for. That's what makes you so beautiful; you've always loved me the way I am and now I realize that and I'm gasping for breath without you. I realize that you are the essential part of me, that my time on this earth is meant to be dedicated to loving you the way you have loved me. And I love you more now than I have at any time because now there are two hearts that are keeping me alive."

It had been ten years since Sherry had heard comparable words from the man she'd exchanged vows and dreams with. "So, you have a near-death experience and today everything is alright? What about tomorrow?"

"I spill my guts to you and you ask me about tomorrow? This is tomorrow." He cleared his throat. "I've had a near-life experience. I've been chasing the wind for the past ten years. Maybe by trying to solve every murder in Forrest, I was trying to fill some void or something. I don't know how you put up with that for so long. Anyway, I've walked away from that part of my life. I want to be a father."

Alarm strained her voice. "You're saying you quit your job?" Silence neither confirmed nor denied her allegation. "What are you going to do now, Walter?"

"I want to be a husband. I want to be there for my son or daughter and I want to be there for you. You've been living through my dreams for the past ten years, now it's your turn." He waited for her to say something. "Hello?"

"I'm still here."

"I want us to start over."

Sherry sighed long and deep. "I don't know. I'm afraid."

"Of what? Me?"

"No, silly. Afraid of failing after starting over."

"I need you to believe in me. Do you still believe in me, Sherry?"

"Yes," she whispered.

"Then we have no need to fear anything." He wheeled right onto Perkins. "I want you to know that I haven't been perfect."

"Neither have I."

Anger ignited in his throat, flamed from his tongue. "What the hell is that supposed to mean?"

"What the hell did you mean when you said it?" she fired back.

He quickly extinguished the potential conflagration. "Nothing. Skip it. I want to see you."

She took her time in answering. "Not now, Walter. I want to think about what I still want, about everything you've said. You sure that accident didn't knock some brains loose or something?"

"Nah, baby. The brains are alright," he laughed. "But I can see a helluva lot better. But listen, you need to stay the hell away from Marcia. That girl—"

"Will you stop that? You know as well as I that she is not gay. And what if she was? You think she'd try to recruit me or something?" She utilized silence as an exclamation point. "So just drop it, alright? I'll talk to you. Soon." She was about to hang up but had an afterthought. "Have you seen your grandmother yet?"

"I'm headed that way now. Hey!"

"What?"

"I'll see you soon, right? And take care of our baby."

"Goodbye, Walter."

Walter, driving through city streets, cut the cell phone off and held it against his lips as if it were a sacred talisman. The sky was darkening by degrees, clouds hovering over the horizon being blown by winds of increasing intensity. He tossed the cell phone out of the window, mashed on the gas. The hell with it. Cell phones, pagers, PDAs. It's all twenty-first-century slavery. Do we seek or are we being led? The more gadgets and gizmos created for convenience, the more alienation and loneliness feeds upon the essence of human nature. Technology and money. Eternal gods of Western civilization; gods of avarice demanding sacrifice of soul and mind. Thanks to technology it's no problem to communicate with someone halfway around the world and so easy to hate, be afraid of or simply not care about the person you're sitting next to on the bus or your neighbor right next door. There are smart bombs, miracle drugs, genetically altered food, but nothing for this estrangement we feel from ourselves, one another, and the worlds we inhabit.

Bryant Towers Housing Project in the daylight was like a woman without makeup. There was no mistaking the scars, blemishes, bags under the eyes, wrinkles. The cover of night provided a cloak against all things grotesque about poverty and unseemliness. That's the thing that makes the ghetto so frightening to outsiders. At night, you know the imperfections are there, but to what degree you'll be exposed to them and when is beyond your control. Night or day, Walter knew where to find his nephew. If he had inhabited the halls of corporate America or offices on Wall Street, Cebo would have been known as a power broker, a mover and shaker. But on the streets the nomenclature player said the same thing in the vernacular of overpriced college degrees. If anything went down in Bryant Towers or the surrounding community, Cebo was in on it. Yes, there were preachers, politicians, businessmen. But one way or another he had to be dealt with also. He knew those people and they knew him, and they knew that his presence had to be recognized or somebody could get hurt. Dope, guns, intimidation were the commodities he bought, sold, traded. There had always been a tacit battle over the hearts of the denizens of Bryant Towers, but recently things had taken a turn even Cebo hadn't imagined. The preachers, politicians, and businessmen had gotten a whiff of federal money in the air and were now in cahoots with the local authorities to eradicate criminal activity from the area. Weed and Seed, they called it. That was before Big Mama Marshall, and since then he had made a peace offering to the legitimate leaders of the community, approaching them with talk of forgiveness and solidarity; but they refused to shake his hand or to acknowledge him at all except behind closed doors. They had heard rumblings of what he had in the works and wanted no part of it or him. That was like an arrow through the heart, and he said fuck you to their faces to hide his hurt.

Cebo seemed to be pondering these things and more, sitting alone on the playground monkey bars, three of his inner circle yards away, thumbing the pages of a book, when he spotted his uncle approaching.

"Well, I'll be damned," shouting with every inch of sarcasm in his body, amazed his uncle was still alive after hearing the full details of his exploits. He beamed from ear to ear, rising to his feet, "Lazarus is a Black man. Man, as long as you're on the job, we don't need no calvary. How you doing, Uncle Walter? People was tellin' me you was dead."

Cebo's inner circle looked admiringly at the display of familial love.

Walter and Cebo held each other in a suspended embrace.

Walter pulled away, trying to conceal the pain in his ribs.

"I'm good, but I've been better." He stood back, arms length, inspecting his nephew from head to foot, as if he hadn't seen him in twenty years. "What's up with you?"

"I'm 'bout to figure it out." Cebo smiled. "Come on into my office." He pointed to the monkey bars and they both squatted their backsides on the matrix of iron metalwork.

He punched his uncle on the knee, beamed again. "You something else, Uncle Walter. You in all the papers, on the news in the streets too, man. You a genuwine regular fucking American hero. All you need now is a white horse and a sunset."

"I just did what I had to do, dogg." A gust of southerly wind kicked up dust and debris; Walter squinted, rubbed the corner of his eye. "Anyway, it's all over now."

Cebo, looking towards the horizon, laughed. "Like I said before, when did white boys start going to jail? You talking 'bout it's all over and they ain't even got no jury together yet." He looked at his uncle with a solemn stare.

"So you admit to sending that fax?"

"Goddam right. I would've sent an email if my goddam hard drive wouldn't've crashed."

"Well, none of that matters now, 'Bo. It's over, 'Bo. The threats, the white boys, it's all over. Nobody walks. The revolution has been cancelled. Permanently."

"Yeah, right. One of 'em might get some time, maybe two. But the one that rolls over on the others might be on the streets right now. And as far as the revolution goes, cancelled? Who cancelled it? The man downtown? Postponed maybe. Besides, as long as there are human beings on the earth, you can't cancel revolution."

There was anger and hostility oozing from Cebo's skin like dime-store cologne.

"You're not being rational, 'Bo. Now as far as one of them boys walking, nah. He'll get a reduced sentence, but he won't walk. That's the way the criminal justice system works, man. I can't do nothing about that."

"I know all about the system. They don't call it criminal for nothing. I've been knowing the system for as long as I've been black. I'm one of the twenty-two million victims of the system, however many Black folks there are in the country. And it's time for the system to go…I don't expect you to do nothing about that. You know, even when you were raising me, I noticed way back then that you always wanted to please everybody. You ever think about putting yourself first sometimes, Uncle Walter?"

"We ain't talking about me."

"I'm not either. I'm talking about us. OK, thangs have been set back for a minute. But it's just a matter of time before some of these skinheads lynch one of us or a cop shoots a Black kid in the back and walks—"

"You wanna riot, 'Bo? That's what you want to do, loot and riot? Burn down your own neighborhood for a few free TVs, malt liquor, and designer sneakers? That's your idea of revolution?"

"Hold on, Uncle Walter. No, that's not what I'm talking about. But if the neighborhood did burn, so what? Everything needs a good cleansing sooner or later. Everybody needs to set fire to something in their lives sooner or later to be free from it. If this neighborhood burned down today it would help the people forget that they were not human beings the way they've been taught to believe they were not. A good fire would kill the nigger in every Black person around here. Besides," he hunched his shoulders, "this block belongs to the Arabs and Koreans now. Go down the street to the store and you'll know what I'm talking about."

"And where in hell do you think you're gonna live then, huh?"

"I ain't sweatin' it. It's the nature of the Black man to survive. That's all I've ever known. Speaking of which," he motioned to one of his homeboys who understood him as if by telepathy, bouncing forward with a book under his arm. Cebo took the book, examined the front cover, tossed it in his hand as if he were weighing the words inside, and handed it to Walter. "We've been studying this."

Walter leaned forward to grab the book. He stared at the picture on the cover of a soldier in battle fatigues and a beret, fanned the pages, stopping to look at the photos inside. Bowing his head, he slammed the book shut, pressed it against his forehead. Che Guevara and guerrilla warfare. Cebo suffered with his uncle in his state of silent anguish for five minutes. Walter raised his head, his face flushed, his nose flaring. "Are you a motherfucking fool? You have completely lost your mind, boy! Don't you know you can't be caught with no shit like this after September eleven? The Feds'll be all over your Black ass for terroristic activities. Throw this shit in the garbage." He held the book as if it were a piece of junk mail looking for a wastebasket.

Cebo's anger rose like a heat flash. "Why don't I just burn it, Uncle Walter? Since when did reading a book become against the law? The hell with September eleven. I read what I want to read and think what I want to think. These white folks running around here thinking everything is alright now, talking about 'we're all Americans now.' Well, what the hell were we before September eleven? They think it's something to always be on guard now. They got a first-hand lesson in what terror is all about. The same way the police, your buddies, have been coming and terrorizing the people of this neighborhood for years. They know what it is to be a nigger now. Hell, I would consider it a compliment if a white motherfucker called me a terrorist, that way I'd know I'm doing something right. He could call me that or anything else he wanted. But my people would call me a freedom fighter."

"Your people? Your people? Man, when things start getting tight these niggers won't even know your name. You won't be nothing but a cold memory, if that. You sound more like a martyr than a freedom fighter. You might not believe it, but I'm your people, 'Bo. Blood people, your mama's brother, and you're not listening to me. Innocent people died in those attacks on September eleven, 'Bo."

"Yeah, innocent people got killed. But think of all the brothers lynched for some bullshit charge of messing with a white woman or Black Wall Street in Tulsa, Oklahoma, in 1921. And don't even mention four little girls on a Sunday morning in Birmingham, Alabama. Or what about all the innocent people around the world who was bombed by US lies and bullets? How come don't nobody never talk about that? Let me tell you what Big Mama taught me when I was a young boy and the times I visited that farm. She said, 'Eric, you plant a apple seed it's just a matter of time before that tree will bear fruit. And it sho won't be a orange.' That was too simple to even think about back then, but now I understand. And the last fucking thing I want to be is a martyr. I want to be around when the real America yields her greatness and pays dividends on top of that so everybody can get paid, not just these white folks."

Walter sat up straight, shook his head and laughed. "You think that'll happen in your lifetime? You might as well strap a bomb to yourself like them fools in the Middle East."

"Ain't no danger. I love life too much. I love it so much I'm willing to die for it. But I get your point and I agree. There ain't no difference between us and the Palestinians. I'm telling you man, its time for these white folks to go."

"I know what I said." Walter gave his nephew a fixed look. "I didn't say there wasn't no difference."

"OK man, chill." Cebo got up and moved closer to his

uncle, wrapped his arm around his shoulder. Walter shoved the book into Cebo's midsection; Cebo took it and laid it on the ground. "I need your help, man." Walter looked skyward and saw lightning rent the evening in two. "Look. I ain't talking about the Palestinians. I'm talking about us. I love you, Uncle Walter and I need you now more than ever."

"You got something to say, say it."

"You mention about us being blood. Well, we need to be more than that. It's time for us to partner up, Uncle Walter. Listen, we got guns, some glocks and nines, assault rifles, shit like that. But we plan on branching out and joining with other brothers all over the country. Thangs will get started here, but it sho in hell won't end here. So, we're gonna need some weapons for long-distance strikes and the way the government is cracking down after September eleven, I thinks I can get my hands on some, I don't know." Walter shook his head in amazement, as if he knew what was coming next. "But what we really need is intelligence. We need somebody on the inside to be on the inside. For us. Diagrams, communications, listening devices. I'm talking the whole nine yards. You know how much damage we could do to this motherfucker?"

Laughter boiled deep within Walter, bubbled in his throat and spilled torridly over the rim of his mouth. He laughed with such fervor that he stood and doubled over, holding his stomach in an effort to stop the mounting mirth. Cebo looked on dumbfounded with a half-smile, half-frown on his face, not wanting to get scalded by the heated hysterics but at the same time desiring to join in. After five minutes of cathartic convulsions, Walter wiped tears from his eyes and stood over his nephew. This kind of laughter was not good for his ribs.

"Intelligence?" He suppressed the hunger for more hilarity. "How goddam stupid is that? I work for the local police department, 'Bo. What you're talking about doing will have you dealing with some shit way over my head... and yours too for that matter. You talking about the National Guard, army, FBI, CIA. That's the only whole nine you're talking about. Let me tell you something," he sat back down on the monkey bars, "I've been on the inside for your little ass for the past five years. Them white boys downtown, my bosses, know who you are and they know who I am and the relationship we've got with one another. It's because of me that they haven't come down on your ass yet. But it's out of my control. God almighty would have a hard time helping you now."

"Is the white man God?" Cebo fired back. "Hell, no. We just need to stop bowing and scrapping at his plastic altars. You give him way too many props, Uncle Walter. Listen, it's all right here, man." He brandished the book in his hand like a torch. "Che has taught us what to do. He left the blueprint right here in this book. Power plants, computers, technology. That's where he is at his strongest and weakest too. You knock out the power to this city or any other major city around this country and you can do whatever in hell you want to. It's a urban war for guerrilla soldiers of four or five to a unit. That's all it takes; it's been proven already. What the fuck the army or CIA gonna do about that? And computers, that's what I'm talking about. That's where you come in. Don't tell me we can't wreak some havoc by hacking into some shit. Hell, we can shut the whole fucking country down that way alone. I ain't no fool, man. I, we, can't take on no whole army or navy; that would be fighting their game. Those days are over with. We want the kind of battle where they don't even know who the enemy is."

"How long did it take you to convince yourself that you wasn't a fool? Where's the intelligence in what you're saying? And consider this right here: yes, the system is screwed, always has been and probably always will be. But as far as I can tell, and this is coming from a Black man, compared to the rest of the other systems around the world, this is the best of the bunch. I mean, goddam, if you did overthrow whatever you're trying to overthrow, what would you replace it with? Nine out of ten, it'll be worse, more oppressive than the one you got rid of. History bears that out…"

"That's bullshit. Cuba is a helluva lot better since Che and Castro led that revolution down there," Cebo blurted.

"That's one country out of how many, 'Bo? And when was the last time you been to Cuba?" Walter sighed, folded his arms across his chest. "All white people are not your enemy, 'Bo. Instead of reading that Guevara crap, you need to read some real history books and then you'll understand what I'm talking about."

It was Cebo's turn to chuckle. His laughter was too bitter to stomach and spat it upon the ground, nodded his head rapidly. "Yeah, I understand. I understand that all white folks ain't the problem. Those white folks that I see protesting the World Bank and IMF or whatever the hell it's call, I ain't got no problem with them. And some of the environmentalists are true revolutionaries too. Hell, we plan on hooking up with all of them one way or the other. But check this right here, Uncle." He used the word 'Uncle' as if it were a sledgehammer aimed at Walter's chest. "Last time you came down here I offered you an opportunity to be with us. But today you come down here and laugh in my face and play me for a sucker and you've made your choice. So peep this: when thangs jump off there'll be only two sides and you're on the wrong one, man. And hey, I guess you're right." He laughed again. "If we got rid of all the white folks in the world, wouldn't nothing change. There'll still be middle-class Negroes to pick up where they left off. In fact those middle-class Negroes would do a better job at being white folks than white folks were ever able to do." He shot a glance at Walter, slanted with innuendo and accusation.

Walter stood, slung the book from Cebo's hand into the dust as thunder boomed overhead and died, repeating itself in the distance.

"Stand up," Walter barked. "The second time around works for me. The first time I came down here, consider yourself blessed. But this time I'm going to beat your ass."

"Uncle Walter, you don't want to do this, man."

"You calling me an Uncle Tom. Stand up and take this ass-whipping like a man, motherfucker."

Cebo's crew stealthily eased behind Walter and around their leader, forming a circle of seven.

"What do you think's gonna happen you try some shit like that? You think I'll let a pig put his hands on me ever again? That's right, I said pig. You've told me where you stand. We're not friends, uncles, nephews, none of that shit." Cebo slowly rose to his feet. "You can't switch hit in the revolution, man. And you telling me you been on the inside for me? I never asked any goddam favors. You know how much of a risk I was taking for talking so close to a cop, uncle or no uncle? But we don't have to worry about that no more. You've made that perfectly clear."

"This between me and you, 'Bo. Call your flunkies off and let's see what you're made of."

"I'm through proving anything to anybody. Step away while you still can!"

"You ungrateful little bastard. I took you in when your own mama didn't even want you. Feed, clothed, housed your little ass..." He lurched forward, was halted by Cebo's men, who grabbed his arms, pinning him to the spot.

There was the nervous agitation of moving feet again, this time from sprinkles of rain drumming in the playground dust. "Alright, I tell you what," Cebo continued, pointing his finger at Walter's chest, "next time I see you I'll stick a fucking medal on your chest and pat you on your goddam back, if that'll make you feel better. But right now, I want you to turn around and bounce the hell up out of here, and while you're leaving you remember this: yes, at one time I ate your food, I wore the clothes you bought, and I slept under your roof. But my thoughts have always been my own. I don't owe you or anybody anything. I'm who I am because I am."

Walter, with a surge of anger and energy, broke the grip of his captors as if he were snapping manacles in two. "Back the fuck off me." He executed a military turn and marched toward his vehicle.

Cebo picked the book out of the dust, wiped specks of mud from Che's picture on the cover, raised it above his head, stood surrounded by his inner circle, all with fists in the air, as the sky ruptured, releasing torrents of rain upon the earth and saturating their shouts of "Viva revolution!"

Rain, finally rain. Walter Robinson relished the sight, sound, smell of it. If the hospital wasn't so far, he would have gladly jumped out of the car and walked the distance to wallow in its wetness, dance in its freshness, and sing of its splendor. Instead, he didn't bother to roll up the windows, flipping his wipers on high, marveling how the rain that fell upon the city wasn't the same rain that burst clouds in the country. As he drove through town, on the edge of nightfall, somehow the rain was strikingly different. In the city it was an irritant turning dirt into grime, altering streets from asphalt into steaming thoroughfares, transforming the air into a blanket of dankness smothering breath and benevolence. Rain on the city delayed its inhabitants with inconvenience and irritation in reaching deadlines and destinations. But it turned the country into fields of green swaying under docile breezes, transformed the air into purified slices of sweet odour and provided a lullaby for the night beneath tin roofs, tapping out distinct rhythms of consolation and soothing. He missed the rain of Big Mama's farm, lying on his back, hands clasped behind head, the radio radiant with pop songs in a far corner of the bedroom and the world pregnant with possibilities at sixteen. At sixteen years old, his world spun on the axis of girls, girls, girls, or older women, Jayne Kennedy, Lynn Whitfield, Pam Grier, running the length of the field as the horn sounded, making the championship basket, barely beating the buzzer, homering in the bottom of the ninth in the seventh game of the series, or owning the baddest, fastest, reddest Corvette ever made, until sleep crept upon you like a thief, stealing fatigue and leaving daybreak like a reward beneath your pillow.

Rain in the city only made the air hotter and the people more discontent. But this was his city, the only one he'd ever known, Forrest, Tennessee. Named after the Confederate general, Nathan Bedford Forrest, who, prior to the war between the states made millions trading in the flesh and misery of human bondage. Forrest, who on an April morning in 1864 slaughtered three hundred Black men, women, and children after they'd surrendered at Fort Pillow overlooking the Mississippi river. Forrest, a founder and president of the KKK from 1867 to 1869, was celebrated with a town named in his honor, the same town that Walter Robinson had come to love and hate at the very same time. Through years of being a cop, murder police, he'd come to know the twists of every alley, fledgling downtown streets and the guarded bars of gated communities. The more things changed in Forrest, the more they didn't. It always will, Walter thought, driving towards the hospital, be a small town with a big-town complex. Yes, there was Double A minor league baseball now, three small liberal arts colleges, and a new city hall. But the town was fueled by the small-minded politics of the segregated South, engineered by the good-old-boy network, middle-aged white men in positions of power making the rules as they go. Three Blacks here or two there or one Black spokesperson for an entire community was always a guarantee that the dynamics of power would never change. Recently, a wave of immigrants had swelled the city's census by nearly ten thousand. At one end of the spectrum were the new rich, CEOs, doctors, retirees, balanced by the Hispanic population, new niggers drifting westward, seeking sustenance from the fertile earth, picking and planting to dusk or rising at daybreak to clean rooms in strange hotels in a English-speaking land generations from nowhere. Mexicans here, Mexicans there, Mexicans everywhere, doing the jobs that white folks think they're too good to do and Black folks feel insulted when asked to do. And the Arab had arrived too, pooling his resources, attaining low-interest loans, setting up shop in the heart of Black communities with corner groceries and gas stations, reassuring customers with unctuous smiles that he was of no relation to Osama and knew nothing of his whereabouts.

But sooner or later, Forrest would arrive, whatever that meant. Eventually, urbanity would come to this dot on the map halfway between two major urban principalities. Walter turned onto West Jackson, came to a stop at a red light, waved at someone who blew at him, advanced. Gangs, drugs, violence were evident in big-city proportions. But there was a paucity of art, culture, intellectual stimulation, and paucity might be an exaggeration at best; in the tradition of fifty years ago, downtown rolled up its sidewalks at five; but there is always the mindlessness of malls. Right now, the refuse from factory chimneys spread over the horizon like a city skyline. But when the steam stopped and the severance pay was parceled, how would the city dig its way out beneath the collapse of economic rubble? Which direction would white flight take this time? In how many more ways would Black hopelessness manifest itself on the east side of town? What would become of his nephew?

Walter maneuvered his car into the hospital's parking garage, making two complete circles before finding a vacant spot on the third level. He sat behind the wheel and thought of Cebo in half-wonder, half-fear. And thoughts of him made him think of Cassandra, Cebo's mother, who at twenty-two decided that she didn't want to be a mother and married any more, fleeing to New York or Chicago or LA, only to be heard from around Christmas and in the occasional birthday card. But none of that mattered now. Cebo was a man. He believed in something, however foolish, enough not only to live for it but to die for it as well. That was more than Walter could say about half the people he knew. Cebo knew what he wanted and he was determined to claim his own glories and accept his own mistakes. Walter knew that Cebo meant what he'd said; that was the way he'd raised him. Come to think of it, Cebo was the sum total of all that Walter had instilled in him, the same thing Grandaddy Marshall had taught him: look a man in the eye when you talking to him, don't say nothing you don't mean and don't take no shit from nobody. Independence was part of his nature. He had simply taken those lessons and was now applying them to his circumstances and situation, however wrong they were. He knew what he wanted from his life, which was more than Walter could say. Right now, he wasn't sure whether he was a cop or a husband or an uncle any more. And he understood Cebo's rage at his country, the sense of being rejected by a birth mother not once but twice. First there's sadness, then pity, and then blind seething rage, hating what you love, hoping to find purpose and meaning having been abandoned in the land of milk and honey when all around you there is pain, poverty, and confusion. As a child he frequently cried over his mother. But as he grew into manhood, his only acknowledgment of her was to dance on her grave.

Walter experienced a mixture of pride and depression. He knew that Cebo wouldn't die over a drug deal or some girl or scuffling over a leather jacket. Those days appeared to be over. In fact, he was surprised that, considering his lifestyle, he hadn't died already. But within the blink of an eye, scales had fallen from Cebo's eyes and the world had become lucid and comprehensible, could be bitten into like succulent red fruit. Cebo was more of a threat now than he ever would be as a gang banger. Gang bangin' was what the system had expected him to do and it was prepared to deal with his actions accordingly, jail or death at the hands of another young Black male being the remedies most often prescribed. He thought of what Lieutenant Peters had said about when a dog goes to take a leak it always raises its leg, and the more he thought about it the more it sounded like some racist's bullshit. Was he equating Black men to dogs, and is that all a Black man knows how to do? Nah. That asshole Ricks maybe, but he considered the lieutenant closer than a friend. But merely to mention the word revolutionary was to threaten the system itself. Instead of drive-bys of indiscriminate shooting, Cebo had a definite target within the cross-hairs of his cold, calculated stare, change being the ultimate bull's-eye. Yes, change, any change. Where the sky sparkles with diamonds by night, children laugh and play because they are innocent and don't know it, and where life is planted in the fertile soil of passion, watered with love and sunshine, and grows to be nurtured for the value of its dignity. If change was destined to be a major disappointment at least the struggle against this life of alienation, helplessness, and broken spirit would have been well worth the blood and sacrifice. Walter knew that either as a gang banger or a revolutionary Cebo was as good as dead. And at that moment he understood that all gang bangers were potential revolutionaries, however misguided, and what the hell kind of society were we living in that created conditions that brought forth such fruit?

Cebo was flesh of his own. Although not to this degree, they'd had fallings out before. He would give him two weeks, a month, to cool down before he'd meet with him again. This time he wouldn't preach, insult or beg; they would meet on the neutral earth of respect and manhood and Walter would accept him just as he was.

Walter pushed opened the door with his left foot and dragged himself from the automobile, cognizant of his damaged ribs and the pain that quick, unexpected movements caused. The only thing more aggravating than the pain was the heat. As soon as he closed the car door and emerged from the parking garage the rain fell upon his head like an answered prayer, and the more he walked the more limber he became. As he approached the hospital's entrance, streetlights winked on. Once he was inside, everyone he passed seemed to have a smile fixed upon their face or a warm hello or a friendly nod of the head, as though they had known him all their lives.

Big Mama was on the sixth floor, transferred from intensive care to a regular room. As a courtesy and out of respect for privacy, hospital staff had removed her name from her door. Walter got into the elevator and a middle-aged white woman, also going up, retreated to the far corner of the elevator and hung onto her purse as if it were a life preserver. He smiled, pushed a button, and felt gravity reverse itself, lifting him upward. Bells chimed as the car came evenly to a stop, its doors opening in hydraulic gusts. She hurried past him, and when Walter uttered, "Have a good night, ma'am," she nearly stumbled out of shock that he hadn't attempted to rob her or that he could actually form thoughts into intelligible words.

Walter got out of the elevator and made his way down antiseptic hallways, past visitors, housekeepers with bent backs and mops in hand, and doctors giving dictation into handheld recorders. He stopped at the nurses' station and was directed to the other end of the hall.

He paced outside of Room 603 until he thought he'd worn the soles from his shoes. He couldn't put it off any more. He had the intestinal fortitude to ram an automobile into another at high speed, but going into that room right now was a helluva lot tougher. He never thought his grandmother would die, let alone be dependent upon tubes, machines, and other people. What would be his reaction and could he control the emotions that would mercilessly demand self-expression? He couldn't remember the last time he had cried or even remembered how to cry. But if he went into that room and it was as bad as he anticipated, remembering how to cry would be the least of his worries; stopping would be his only problem then. He took a deep breath, released it quickly, and lunged into the room as if someone had both hands in his lower back and was pushing him.

Inside the room the television emitted low tones from an overhead shelf, open drapes still allowing thunder and intermittent flashes of lightning to clumsily prowl through the windows. Big Mama lay on her back, eyes closed, with an IV in one arm and her breasts rising and falling like consecrated offerings. He tiptoed towards the bed, its head elevated at a forty-five-degree angle, beside it a bedside table with a gold water pitcher and matching tray, a reclining chair, and the hum of an air conditioner. Her hair was in two long braids and there were bruises and scratches on her face and arms. Sleeping deeply and peacefully, she looked as though she'd aged ten years. Walter stood over his grandmother and shook his head, not out of sadness, but out of sheer wonder. Her strength and resolve were amazing. She had been determined to make it to her neighbor's house a half-mile away. She had taken two bullets, tried to stand, and instead crawled out of the front door, down the driveway and out into the road before collapsing into the arms of night. Thomas Pickering, who was on his way back to town, wrapped her in blankets and dialed 911 on his cell phone.

He had always worried about his grandmother staying alone in the isolated farm since Grandaddy died three years ago. He had went to the chicken coop like he did most mornings to gather fresh eggs for breakfast, and after a two-hour delay, Big Mama found him lying on his back, the basket of broken eggs by his side; the coroner ruled it heart attack. Walter had taken as many safeguards as possible to protect her since then: motion lights, security doors, caller ID; she had refused bars on the window, fearing not being able to escape fire, and a burglar alarm because who in the devil would hear it way out there? And coming to live with himself and Sherry was out of the question. She had told him that the farm had been a good enough place for her husband to take his final breath, and that...well...his spirit was still on the place and to sell it would be a sin. Walter's heart couldn't argue with that, even though his head told him otherwise.

But she definitely would need someone to look after her now. For the next month or longer he didn't have a damn thing to do and some quite time in the country would do them both good. She had dedicated the formative years of his youth to admonishing and nurturing and now he would repay her, not out of duty or sentiment but with the one thing she had given him: love. And Sherry could live with them too. And baby makes four. And don't forget Grandaddy. Fresh eggs, fresh air, a fresh start, away from the hard edge of the city. Right now Big Mama was all he had.

Walter moved towards the window, slid the drapes together. He bent over his grandmother, planted a kiss on her forehead, hesitated before turning for the door.

"Walter? Walter, that you?"

Her voice was as feeble as a plea.

Walter was back at her bedside, stroking her hand in his, more hugs and kisses. "Hey, Big Mama. Yeah, it's me. You feeling better?"

She leaned forward in bed, trying to get a closer look. A smile stretched her face, forcing tears to spill over the edges of her eyes. "There's my Walter Lewis. I thought you'd forgotten all about Big Mama. Sherry has been here. Even Eric. How you doing baby?" She scrutinized him. "You're soaked, baby."

He had resolved not to let his emotions get the better of him and he tried to fall back on an old police tactic in order to maintain control. Whenever he was investigating an extremely horrific crime—like the time two youths went on an angel dust binge and two days later had slaughtered an infant, ripping out its heart and masticating it, claiming the babe was the lamb of God—Walter had to force himself to have an out-of-body experience to solve the crime, not take it home with him and most of all to preserve his sanity. But this time on the sixth floor at the county hospital, no matter how many buttons he pushed, it wouldn't work. There were no tricks he could play to convince himself that he wasn't really here or that this had never happened to him, and against his better judgment and will he felt his vision blur with tears and his breath become tangled within his chest.

"Don't cry, Big Mama." He kissed the tears running down her cheeks, the way she used to kiss his scraped wounds from running and falling as a kid out in the country. "It's gonna be alright. You're asking about me when I should be asking about you. But don't worry, I won't let anyone hurt you ever again. I'll die first."

His words triggered a sense of remembrance that reflected a stare from her eyes, vacant and penetrating. Walter could see the fear and confusion. He hugged and rocked her until she relaxed on his bosom, saying, "My Walter Lewis, my Walter Lewis."

Big Mama laid back upon the bed, holding Walter's hand in hers. She smiled, no longer crying, and looked deeply into her grandson's eyes. Slowly her smile dissipated and her brow furrowed. She sighed heavily, as if there was a pain in her chest.

"I'm so tired, baby. Pray for me, Walter Lewis."

"Alright," he smiled, shifting his weight from one foot to the other, wondering what she was seeing as she looked at him. "Alright, Big Mama. I'll pray for you."

She shook her head. "No. I mean right now."

She closed her eyes, readying for the words to fall from his lips in supplication and when she reopened them he stared at her as if she had all the answers.

"Pray, boy, pray."

He tried to make his lips fit around the right words only managing to form half-syllables, like a sinner stuttering before the judgment seat of God. He closed his eyes, but that only served to exacerbate his futility, words floating into darkness beyond the reach of his entreaty.

Finally, he capitulated, opened his eyes and, gently placing his grandmother's hand by her side, averted his face from hers. "I don't know the words any more, Big Mama. I'm sorry." He wanted to run from the room.

"Lord have mercy. My baby hurtin' so bad. You gotta find them words Walter Lewis. If you wanna live, you gotta find them words. Don't just find them for me. You gotta find them for yourself. If you don't, you can't find your place in this world, you ain't got no place in this world." She raised herself up on her elbows. "He ain't went off and left you. I'm talkin' 'bout the God that you knew when you used to rip and run out on the farm when you was a kid. The God of Sunday school and the one you used to ask to bless your food and to watch over as you slept through the night. He ain't changed a lick and He ain't forgot your name." She laid back down. "Lord, I'm so tired, Walter Lewis." Big Mama turned, faced the window exhausted from thought and word.

Walter kissed her goodbye on her cheek, stopped with the door half open. "I know, Big Mama. Get some rest now."

"You don't have to apologize to me."

He hushed her with a shake of his head. "I'll see you in the morning."

From Big Mama's room to the elevator was the longest walk Walter had ever taken in his life. He felt small, impotent, and broken. He waited for the elevator to pull its weight up from the basement. When the doors opened, the car was empty, and as he stepped inside he made up his mind to stop by the emergency room to get checked out. He pushed a bank of buttons on the left, initiating the elevator's downward flight, its doors closing in upon him like a sepulcher. He fell to the elevator's floor upon his knees and, hands clasped, eyes directed skyward, cried, "Forgive my unbelief. O God, forgive my unbelief!"

Joe Hardegree stood on the front porch, checked over both shoulders for signs of anyone following him or lurkers around corners. After an extended sigh of relief, he walked into his home with a sack of groceries in one hand and the keys that he had unlocked the door with in the other. He had cut another day and was once again thankful for being able to hear the voices of those most dear to him. Immediately he was attacked by Michael and Hannah screaming at the top of their lungs, one at the waist, and the other at the knees, as if he were Santa during the first minutes of Christmas morning. He pleaded for momentary release, wrapped his arms around his wife Deanna, and kissed her like a soldier returning home from war. She was adorned in a red-and-white apron and brown sandals. After coming up for air, she thanked him, with a surprised look on her face, for stopping by the store to pick up tomato sauce, bread and milk for Hannah, then launched her own interrogation concerning the origins of stains on his recently laundered pants.

He kissed her again, said you're welcome with a pinch on her behind, and mentioned a day in the life of a homicide detective. She blushed, admonished him about the kids watching, and playfully shoved him away.

Joe turned around and found both offspring standing there with smiles of anticipation.

"Alright, kids. Let's go for a ride!" He heard Deanna cautioning in the background that supper would be served shortly.

He sat on the couch, a child on each knee, held tight to their shirttails, bounced both legs up, down, and sideways and shouted, "And they're off!" over the screams of glee, shouts of pure ecstasy from two jockeys in pursuit of imagination and joy, coming down the home stretch before supper and bubble baths, then to be tucked beneath the warmth of bedtime stories and goodnight kisses. Later, Joe Hardegree would awaken at two in the morning and steal away to the kids' room to watch them sleep. It was good to be home.